THE ADULTERANTS

Joe Dunthorne

HAMISH HAMILTON
an imprint of
PENGUIN BOOKS

HAMISH HAMILTON

UK | USA | Canada | Ireland | Australia
India | New Zealand | South Africa

Hamish Hamilton is part of the Penguin Random House group of companies
whose addresses can be found at global.penguinrandomhouse.com.

First published 2018
001

Copyright © Joe Dunthorne, 2018

The moral right of the author has been asserted

Printed in Great Britain by Clays Ltd, St Ives plc

A CIP catalogue record for this book is available from the British Library

ISBN: 978–0–241–30547–8

www.greenpenguin.co.uk

For Maya

PART ONE

'. . . And I think it's a problem with our idea of innocence,' she said, and it was clear from the changeable volume of her voice that we were having one of the most engaged conversations at 8b Longford Close. My wife, Garthene, was not at the party. She was not about to emerge from the bathroom and discover her husband reaching a windy philosophical plateau with an unmarried woman who, from a distance, seemed to be wearing a lot of poorly applied lipstick but in reality just had an unusual upper-lip transition.

'You should speak to my wife,' I said. 'Garthene loves this kind of thing.'

It is terrific to have a partner with the name Garthene. Just the mention of it brings decorum to a conversation.

'Funny,' she said, 'you don't look married.'

I spotted Dave Finlay and waved him over. Dave, one of the top focus pullers in the UK film industry, was travelling back from the kitchen with a pile of crisps in his cupped left hand, a full glass of wine in his right. The accuracy of movement required by a focus puller is incredible. Garthene and I reckon Dave Finlay for a very precise lover. It is okay for us to joke about this because Garthene could never find Dave attractive on account of one of his habits. When he drinks wine, small beads of it become trapped in the thick hairs of his moustache, and Dave is aware this happens, so after each sip he draws his bottom lip up over his top lip and pulls down remnants of, in this instance, Picpoul de Pinet. What I'm fairly certain Dave doesn't know is that this creates a flick-back whereby his moustache, as it regains its shape, spritzes a very fine, near-imperceptible mist of what we can safely assume is a mix of wine and mouth juices. The spray does not so much land on anyone as just *become one* with the atmosphere in the room, reminding us that the air we breathe is full of each other's fluids and innards and skin. In the abstract, I have no problem with knowing this. When we smell something we absorb tiny bits of that smell's source. Fine. But Garthene and I agree that, in the moment of a conversation with Dave Finlay, becoming aware that your next in-breath will be, to a greater than normal extent, rich in his DNA, is a pretty profound turn-off. I wondered whether the situation would get easier if Dave kept a neater moustache, but before that could happen he would need the self-respect engendered by an active love life, and before that could happen he would need a neater moustache, and so on.

The unmarried woman shook the raised pinky of Dave's wine-holding hand, introduced herself, then touched his elbow, which was my cue to drift away. I went into the bathroom and composed a message for my wife. *The stench of death, Garthene. The stench of death overwhelming this whole charade. Every clinked glass, every hollow laugh, every rewind – the more noise we make, the easier the black wing finds us in the dark. The canapés also, bullshit. 6/10.*

We don't have friends who make canapés. The gap in meaning would be obvious to my wife. Garthene would want me to have a good time but would appreciate my pretending not to, since she was working nights. She texted back: *Drink more x.* That felt good because my wife does not *x* lightly.

Back in the corridor, Michael Bonner was dabbing at his phone, waiting to go into the toilet after me. Nobody resented Michael for still being into cocaine because we all understood that, for him, the bathroom was a kind of time machine. He would come out a few minutes later looking startled, having visited himself at a house party from five years ago, before he had met Kamara and had twin girls. I knew from experience to avoid Michael until much later on in the evening, when his drugs had run out and he hated himself a little. Then he became quite likeable.

On my wife's advice, I quickly finished my large glass of wine before heading back into the lounge. There, Lee, our host, was preparing drinks. I watched him rhythmically slam a tea towel full of ice cubes against the edge of the dining table. An ineffective way to crush ice but undeniably impressive. In the kitchen, I found his wife, Marie – very beautiful, with a high forehead and good wrinkles – lighting a cigarette off the hob. I knew it was not a problem for Garthene, my talking to Marie. Marie and Lee have always carried an air of tremendous financial-sexual security. It's also clear Marie has spent her whole adult life being the attractive person and finds it not exactly boring, just unworthy of comment. She waved away the smoke as I approached.

'Ray,' she said, 'great you're here.'

I made an exaggerated play of sucking in the second-hand smoke and she laughed silently, which made what was left in her lungs come out. Strange how different it felt, taking in Marie's exhalations compared to the mouth juices of Dave Finlay. She hopped up on to the counter to blow smoke more accurately out of the narrow window. Her bare calves on the white handle-free cabinet were pretty special. I knew that Garthene would think it weird for me *not* to notice them. Not registering them would be a sign that I was too frightened to look for fear of combusting with repressed lust. Her legs were outstanding. That was no problem. She had a semicircle-shaped scar that made her left kneecap look cheerful.

'I've been the pace car this evening, Ray.'

'I hadn't noticed.'

'My husband sent me here to take a long slow drink of delicious water.'

'You seem sober. I'd put you in charge of heavy machinery.'

'Lee says I'm too old for this. Too old to make it work.'

'You have one of those faces that never look drunk. Try slurring something.'

She looked down at her lap. 'Gnsh um chuffly.'

'There you go,' I said.

'Undla spurdoon.'

'Great. Now you're more convincing.'

She smiled and squinted at me through the smoke. 'You *are* starting to seem good-looking,' she said.

This was fine, by the way. Garthene could have been in the room with us and it would not have been an issue.

'I worry the wine has compromised an authentic sense of your own agency,' I said. 'So it's morally impossible for us to sleep together.'

'But what if the wine has just allowed me access to my true feelings?'

'As a modern man, I make no assumptions. I'd need very clear signals. I will literally never assume anything about anyone, that's how modern I am.'

'What if I dragged you upstairs?' she said.

'Well, I'd lie completely still on the bed, make no movements whatsoever, and if you chose, of your own volition –'

'Then you'd let me feed on you?'

'Then I would facilitate your needs.'

'Lucky Garthene.'

The mention of my wife's name was proof, if any were needed, that she had been implicitly in the room throughout the preceding exchange. Marie handed me her cigarette because she knows that, after a few drinks, I have a fondness for the third quarter. There was lipstick on the filter. She was not wearing lipstick that looked like she was wearing any, but here it was.

Lee came in with two drinks. 'Is the pace car on blocks yet?' he said.

Marie pulled a used pint glass from the sink, filled it with tap water and necked the lot, her throat pulsing, a dribble running into the hollow of her left collarbone. She was breathing hard by the time she brought the pint down. They had a little stare-off, then he nodded and put a tall fizzy drink next to her thigh on the counter. She watched it release carbon dioxide into the atmosphere. He gave the other drink to me.

'You're a gent,' I said.

I had enjoyed my conversation with Marie so much I felt like staying in the kitchen and talking more. Lee watched me hand the cigarette back to his wife. He leaned against the cooker.

'Why isn't Garthene here?' Lee said.

'She's on nights,' I said. 'Won't finish till six in the morning.'

'That's okay,' Lee said. 'We won't be asleep.'

'Even so, she has a thing about the way she smells after a night shift,' I said. 'Toxin sweat. I try to tell her it's the scent of dedicating one's life to the care of others, but she says that's exactly the sort of thing someone who's not spent time in a hospital would say.'

Neither of them was listening. Lee watched Marie light another cigarette. She was usually just a social smoker but tonight she'd upgraded. I could hear one of the hobs hissing as Lee's backside pressed against the dials. His head got redder as he drank. He was a few shades shy of full ripeness now. Marie blew smoke at him and he stared at her through it then turned and asked me to look after her before shouldering back into the lounge. I reached over and turned off the hob.

'He's a good man, your man,' I said.

Marie stopped bothering to aim her cigarette smoke out of the window.

'Can I ask you something?' she said.

'Anything.'

'Has Garthene told you about my and Lee's arrangement?'

'I don't think so.'

'Then your wife sure can keep a secret,' she said, and she laughed.

The air in the room was changing colour.

'So what's the arrangement?' I asked.

'That we're both allowed to sleep with one stranger a year.'

'You're kidding.'

'I am not kidding,' she said. 'And basically that means —'

'Hang on,' I said, holding up my hand. '*Every* year?'

'Well, because the way —'

'What if you're together for, like, thirty years?' I said. 'That's two football teams and all the coaching staff.'

When I think of a decent joke I just have to make it.

Marie was silent. We could hear Michael Bonner in the next room making a strong case for something.

'Ignore me,' I said. 'I'm a terrible listener. So you can sleep with anyone you want to?'

'Not exactly. There *are* rules. It can't be a friend and it has to happen outside London.'

'Makes sense,' I said. 'Because anything that occurs beyond the M25 has no consequence, ethically or emotionally.'

'There you go,' Marie said.

'How do you keep track of who's done what and how often?'

'We don't,' she said. 'The point is: never talk about it.'

I shook my head in awe.

'We trust each other to lie to each other,' she said.

'You two are so futuristic.'

We could see Lee in the lounge picking up and putting down beer cans on the coffee table until he found one he liked the weight of.

I had not noticed Marie finishing her drink but it was finished.

'Let's go upstairs,' she said.

At Marie and Lee's parties, the spare room tended to be an overflow space, but tonight it was empty. There was a prince-size bed in the middle of the room, a dresser to one side, and a winged armchair to the other. Marie propped up the pillows and got under the duvet with her back against the padded headboard. She lifted the edge of the covers and I went around the bed and got in beside her. We didn't take off our shoes, which made a difference, morally. The room was well lit and the built-in mirrored wardrobe allowed us to observe ourselves. It was an amusing sight, Marie fully clothed in bed, smoking luxuriously. I enjoyed the situation. On one wall there was a clip-framed architectural blueprint. On my side the ceiling slanted down with the roof. Marie's right hand held the cigarette while her left hand rested under the covers, next to my leg.

I made an attempt to imagine Garthene in the room with us. Garthene, sober and returning from the night shift, smelling of bacterial emissions, putting one hand on the door frame for balance as she slipped off her shoe. Her husband and her oldest friend's wife smoking in a small double bed. I realized that the situation was defined by my feelings about it. If I regarded this moment as sexually meaningful, that's what it became. But if my main concern was how my wife would interpret these circumstances, then the situation was not inherently hurtful and only worrying because of how it might be misconstrued. I was able to disarm the whole enterprise with the power of clear thinking.

Marie passed me her cigarette as it got towards the good bit. In the mirror, we looked post-coital but sad, as though we'd started having sex but one of us had encountered a problem – *I just can't do this, sorry* – so we'd given up and were now merely running through our private neuroses in silence.

'Do you want to know what else?' she said.

'Very much,' I said.

'Lee *thinks* I sleep with other people but I don't. I don't sleep with anyone except him.'

In the mirror I watched my own eyebrows rising.

'So there you go,' she said. 'Shame on me. I have been utterly faithful.'

'You mean you made the arrangement but you haven't ever actually . . . ?'

'That's my dark secret. And I just can't seem to enjoy him fucking other people either.'

Through the floorboards there came the bark of Michael Bonner laughing.

The door opened a fraction, Dave Finlay's head appeared, then he apologized, retreated.

Marie looked into my eyes via the mirror. It was comfortable this way; we could look at each other with only the slightest adjustment of our normal gaze. It meant that we weren't turned towards each other in bed, which would have crossed a line, I decided, since our eyes and mouths would have been too close together. Even with clothes and shoes on, turning towards each other in a prince-size bed was a definite line. The duvet cover's pattern was the flag of Japan, a country famous for youth suicide. When I passed the cigarette back to Marie, she reached for it awkwardly with her right hand. She kept her left hand where it was, under the duvet, gently knuckling my thigh. I could feel her wedding ring.

I looked into her eyes in the mirror while she blew smoke out and, for a moment, we both looked black and white. We travelled through time. When Marie first arrived in our friendship group, there had been a little jousting among the single men, until she and Lee got together. I was not one of the guys involved. I just can't get excited about someone who doesn't have some pretty promin-ent flaws.

From downstairs, we could hear the gush of nitrous balloons inflating. The evening had reached its next stage. In the early days of our romance, Garthene used to steal canisters of Entonox from work and bring them to parties. There was the thrill of the drug itself and, equally powerful, the thrill of wasting public-health resources.

We heard Lee coming up the stairs. He was talking to the unmar-ried woman. She was saying: 'I'm getting a whiff of aspiration from your art collection, Lee.'

'Glad to hear it. Wouldn't want Marie to have spent all that money and have nobody notice.'

Lee paid Marie rent. He was a tenant husband, which was very modern. Marie was the only one of our friends who owned prop-erty, though Garthene and I were trying. Just the month before, we'd had our hearts broken, gazumped on a nasty little split-level in the dead land at the edge of Walthamstow Marshes. Now we were waiting to hear about our asking-price offer on a horrible maisonette beyond the Lea Bridge roundabout.

I felt the mattress shift as Marie yelled for her husband. 'Leebo!' she said. 'Leebo!'

'Yes, dear,' he called through the door.

'Ray and I are in bed here and absolutely parched.'

I thought it was important to be part of the joke. Some jokes only carry if everyone gets behind them. 'It's true, big man. Me and your wife have got a major thirst on.'

'I'm just showing my new friend your flat,' he said. 'She wants to judge you and it can't wait.'

The woman spoke through the door: 'Lee's right, Marie. I've been putting off these generalizations for quite long enough.'

It was good that everyone was getting on board.

As we heard them go into the master bedroom next door, Marie's hand moved on top of my thigh and nudged the edge of my crotch. She blew smoke up towards the paper lampshade. As long as I did not turn towards her, it was fine. I was helping Marie through a difficult moment in her marriage. And with that thought, I brought Garthene into the room with us. Garthene, who knows more than most about putting herself in challenging situations for the health and happiness of others, was in the room, wearing her purple nurse's tunic, and she gave a solemn nod.

You cannot blame a body. That was one thing her job had taught her. You cannot blame a body for its response.

Marie was looking at me without use of the mirror — she had turned her head. Her hand was on my crotch, which had responded without my say-so.

'You dream about me, don't you?' she said.

'I do,' I said, 'absolutely.' It was important to work through this.

'You dream about me.'

'It's true.'

My sex dreams were unique because if I made love to a woman who was not my wife, I would usually experience in-dream remorse. I would seek to apologize, in the dream. I felt Marie's hand tighten and she yelled at the wall: 'Lee, thirsty work in here.'

We listened to the conversation stop next door. Their voices lowered then carried on.

'How's Garth?' Marie said.

It was good to know we could still bring my wife into the conversation.

'She's great.'

'I bet she looks fantastic naked right now, doesn't she?'

'She does.'

Then the door opened and Lee came in. His face was its deepest colour and he had a bottle of rum in his hand. I let my left leg slip out from under the cover just so he could see I had my shoes on. It was too deliberate, I now realize.

'He-ey, party in here,' he said, and he stepped up to the bed and unstopped the bottle. He handed the rum to his wife, then his face came swooping down and he kissed me on the lips and laughed. 'We're lucky you've got things under control,' he said, then he tried to kiss me with tongues but my mouth wasn't fully open so his tongue hit my teeth. Then he laughed harder, with his head thrown back. I tasted rum. His neck was bright pink and showing the cords beneath.

'Wahey!' he said and took the bottle from his wife and drank.

I slipped out of bed sideways and stood where the ceiling of the room slanted down. I had to crouch slightly, which was a useful position for me. Lee crawled over the bed into the warm patch where I had been and kissed his wife. His shirt rode up. We were not the kind of friendship group who valued muscles, which made his commitment to them all the more remarkable. He kissed Marie and reached under the covers between her legs. Then he came over to where I was crouching and put his hand towards my face, and I thought he might hit me so I winced. He just dragged the wet side of his finger along my upper lip.

I slid along the wall, my back hunched over, mouth-breathing. I understood that to take in the smell would be to receive Marie's private secretions. The line would be long gone if I inhaled through my nose.

Lee reached down and prodded the lump in the crotch of my trousers. He pressed it like a doorbell. 'Ding-dong!' he said.

If Garthene were here.

'Ding-dong!' He poked my crotch-lump then laughed.

Marie was watching herself in the mirror.

I manoeuvred along the built-in wardrobe towards the door. In all likelihood I was absorbing tiny Marie particles anyway, becoming minutely contaminated, so I wiped my upper lip with my sleeve. Lee saw that and his jaw hardened. I thought he was going to hit me, which he did. The first was in the mouth and, although he punched in a way that didn't seem especially powerful – because Lee was standing a little far back, he had to take two steps as he swung, had to carry his fist across the room – he still connected and my mouth filled with the taste of coins. Then it made sense that Lee, having felt, I think justifiably, that the first punch had not been satisfying, took a wide stance, set his feet, bent his knees, and – with his wife behind him saying something along the lines of 'Oh, come on', as though his behaviour were nothing more than a little impolite, like hogging the binoculars at the opera – had another go. I believe the phrase is *I saw it coming from last week*. Time slowed or, to be more accurate, it gained texture. We retain more detail about traumatic events. No surprise that those few

seconds between the first punch and the second have come to stand
in for probably three months of my thirties. That I had never been
punched in the face before seemed faintly ridiculous. How could
I claim full maturity without ever having jumped through that life
hoop? There were the obvious feelings you'd expect – pain, shock,
fear that my average looks could not carry off a characterful nose –
but also pride that I no longer held the burden of innocence, this
virgin face, and relief, too, at being damaged, because that was
realistic, that was something to build on, and so I hoped for minor
disfigurement, not anything massive but a cute little scimitar-
shaped blue-white ridge of scar tissue working with the shape of
my cheekbone, something to mark my arrival in adulthood, and I
remember thinking I could have dodged the second punch, could
have ducked or weaved so that he would have hit the mirror, which
would have cracked, and he would have been left looking at a
fractured vision of his wife and himself, sliced into thirds by a knife
so sharp they could not feel the blade pass through and it might
have been the kind of metaphor that can save a marriage – seeing
himself with bleeding knuckles, Marie trapped in a web of shattered
glass – and things might have ended differently, but he connected
sweetly, and in that moment before I blacked out, I knew there
must have been great satisfaction in finding my left eye socket,
which I should say was a tremendous home, shape-wise, for the
adult male fist.

If you have ever walked in public covered in blood you will know
it is a wonderful feeling. I drank from the bottle of rum and texted
my wife in the bluegrass style: ♪ *Walkin' the streets / taste o' blood
in my mouth / on my way to see my wo-man* ♫.

I entered Homerton Hospital with the bottle in my sock. In the
busy waiting room, there was a young couple crying and holding

hands on the easy-wipe chairs. He was so tall and she so tiny I couldn't help feeling they had got together not from any profound attraction so much as an instinct for the perverse. Everyone else was sitting politely with their avoidable injuries, waiting for a free dose of medium-grade healthcare, completely unaware that outcomes go way downhill on the weekend.

'Head wounds,' I said, stepping up to the reception desk, 'always look worse than they are.'

'Name, please?'

I gave her my details, knowing, because Garthene had told me, that now I was registered with the receptionist a communal file would be created with notes on my condition (*query: drunk?*) and if her colleagues recognized my name, they might contact her and, if she found me in A&E, I would have to explain myself in public, which would invoke her terrifying professional voice. I knew that in order to give my wife a fair and nuanced picture of why I was bleeding from the face, I would need to speak to her alone, deploy the full range of irony, theatre, special pleading. That meant getting out of A&E and visiting her ward.

At the edge of the room, I located an ethanol gel dispenser. Garthene had taught me the correct way to clean one's hands – concentrating on the tips of fingers, not the palms – and I felt this motion lent me authority. I moved towards the double doors that led into the hospital proper, pretending to take an interest in the painting hanging nearby. Local artists donated their work, this one a sunny acrylic of the Mare Street bus depot. There was a clear sense the artist had enjoyed creating it, which I found embarrassing. In the reflection in the plastic glass, my bloody lip and half-closed eye brought a needed sense of conflict to the work.

'Omar Badji . . . Carla Montemaggiore.' Nurses kept calling unusual names.

As the receptionists turned to look towards a sharp cry of agony from the woman in the mismatched couple, I took my chance – pushing through the rubber-edged doors into the corridor beyond, into the hospital smell of bleach and potatoes. Many parts of the building, I knew, were empty at this time, and security under-staffed. A few weeks ago they had found students on temazepam jellies riding tricycles through the Diabetes Centre. I walked with purpose over the pale linoleum, finishing off the rum, following the signs to the Intensive Care Unit. I know it's not a competition, but I like to tell people my wife works on the scariest ward. Heart failures, pneumonias, road accidents, suicide attempts. *ICU makes A&E look like a fucking wellness spa* is the sort of thing I say. Once the bottle of rum was empty, I dumped it in a red pedal bin marked *Offensive Waste*.

When I got to ICU, I looked through the strip of reinforced glass. There were two nurses at a station in the middle of the dark-ened ward, facing each other, like a dinner date. I buzzed the intercom and positioned myself so the camera would only see the good half of my face, the unswollen zone.

'Who's that?' the nurse whispered.

'It's Ray. Garthene's husband.'

'Oh, Ray. The man of the moment. To what do we owe the pleasure?'

'A spontaneous act of romance,' I said.

'Aw, young love,' the nurse said.

'I'm nearly thirty-four,' I said.

'Aw, middle-aged love,' she said. 'But you know she's on her sleep break.'

'Darn,' I said. 'I'll just wait.'

'That's sweet,' the nurse said, sounding impressed, then, pre-sumably talking to her colleague: 'He'll wait.'

I went down the corridor and stood outside the staff coffee room where Garthene and her colleagues took naps. I put my ear to the door but could hear nothing. It was bad form to disturb her, but it felt vital to deliver the news now while the wounds were still bleeding. I ran my tongue around the hatch of split flesh inside my mouth. Everything in there seemed massive. Since I probably still had some residual Marie microbes on my upper lip, I used another ethanol gel dispenser and smeared a little in the space where my moustache would grow, if I could grow one. Inhaling through my nose, I enjoyed the light-headedness, and while that feeling was with me gripped the coffee room's door handle. I made a point of turning it fully so that the bolt did not clip the escutcheon. I was careful in that loud way of drunk people trying to be quiet. I slipped through narrowly, closed the door, then stood in the dark and the warmth, listening to the sound of breathing, the spooky low hoot of my wife's congested sinuses. There was the scent of bad coffee and hot shoes and, deeper than that, sick people's night sweats and particulates being exhaled, death gusts swirling the room.

As I was waiting for my eyes to adjust, a phone shone in the darkness. It was Garthene's, vibrating silently. I had recommended she keep the handset's microwave radiation away from our unborn child, but it was right beside her. It up-lit her bump. I saw a backlog of texts. There was my message in the bluegrass style and then three from Lee: *need to speak to you / i'm a fuckup / please call xxx*. In the phone's diffuse blue glow, I could see she was on her side on a low sofa, had a pillow under her head and another between her thighs.

I wanted to wake Garthene in a peaceful way. If her body produced adrenaline it would travel down the umbilical cord and create panic in the foetus. Stressed mothers produce stressed babies. Some pregnant women avoid current affairs altogether, delete the newspapers from their phones. Happily, Garthene and I had always maintained a high level of political disengagement.

I got out my phone and rang my wife, at the risk of increasing local radiation. One of those moral compromises for which parenthood is famous. Her phone lit up, shuffled beside her on the sofa cushion, and she shifted in her sleep. I could just make out two other nurses, one man, one woman, lying across padded chairs on either side of the room. The man, I noticed, was very tall, unable to stretch out on the seats, resting his head on his hands. It occurred to me that he had given his pillow to my wife and I felt a mixture of gratefulness and rage. It seemed important to know whether his pillow was the one under her head or the one between her legs. I rang her again and watched her shoulders stiffen, her fingers contract. She was swimming up through layers of consciousness.

They had these sleep breaks every night shift and if she always clamped *his* pillow between her thighs, let it marinate there, soaking up the gonadotropins, then did that not cross a line? I tried to become outraged. If she was having an affair, then that made my indiscretion with Marie laughably slight. *To think I came here to apologize when in fact you are the evil one* was a pleasant sentence, and I let it bob around behind my eyes a moment before calling her number again.

On the sixth ring, I watched Garthene reach for the phone and look at it, her eyes half closed, puffy and luminous in the screen light. It was a unique experience to see her unguarded expression while receiving my call at three in the morning. She squinted at the phone as it rang two more times before placing it gently on the floor, face down. Perhaps it was not even my child, I thought. Perhaps it was the love child of my wife and her colleague.

'Garthene,' I whispered. 'Garthene.'

*

Throughout our twenties, nobody in our friendship group had been willing to admit they wanted to procreate. It was a shameful, secret pursuit, like skiing. From the age of eighteen to thirty-five, Garthene had taken the combined pill. We used to joke that she had all her unused eggs backed up inside her, and if she ever did come off the pill they'd all come barrelling down at once with a rumbling sound, like when you release the balls on a pub pool table. Then Michael and Kamara's twins broke the deadlock. The first day we met them they dozed on our laps, pinned us to our chairs with happiness. *Garthene, I think I want one.* She said she needed more time. She still felt too young. I made the point that, in the eyes of modern medicine, a thirty-five-year-old mother is officially geriatric. And anyway, there was a nine-month inbuilt waiting time, not to mention the whole conception palaver, which could easily take half a decade, particularly given my lifestyle. All those years with my laptop on my actual lap. Hot baths. Tight trousers. Everything pointed towards a devastated sperm count. Instinctively, I just did not *feel* fertile. I got myself tested. It turned out that I had a low sperm count but excellent morphology and motility. Quality, not quantity. Garthene came off the pill, not because we were going to try for a baby straight away but just to check that she too had a healthy reproductive system. Baby steps towards baby steps. We bought a fertility-tracking app called Ovulator. Each morning it asked Garthene whether her cervical mucous resembled water, raw egg white or school glue. This was a new intimacy, knowing my wife's inner texture, updated in real time. It messaged us with :-) on a fertile day and :-(on the infertile ones. Garthene disapproved of the regressive suggestion that people without children are not happy. I disapproved as well, while privately fearing it true. We had unprotected sex only on the sad days and, just once, very drunk on duty-free schnapps, on a happy day, after which Garthene was immediately pregnant. One and done. Garthene took the news badly. Since drinking alcohol was inadvisable, she went for long walks alone, out across the marshes, gloveless even though it was January, coming back with her hands turned to claws, eyes streaming. For a week, she slept only in two-hour blocks as though road-testing future sleep deprivation. I told her that I would absolutely respect and support her decision, whether she wished to go ahead with the pregnancy or terminate it, and, with this display of loving maturity, I was building a case for myself as a father.

*

Sitting alone beside the nurses' station in ICU, I held an antiseptic gauze to my mouth and waited for Garthene. She had broken hospital protocol to let me sit here outside visiting hours. It felt good to be an exception. The ward was dark and calm, just the sound of soft footsteps and ventilators steadily wheezing, the occasional bleat of an IV alarm. It had the atmosphere of a long-haul night flight – low light, interrupted sleep and a psychotic trust in machines. A sign on the wall said *Shhhh* because noise, particularly human voices, can be stressful in the drugged and paranoid half-dreams of patients on the border of life and death. It occurred to me only now that there were few places less appropriate for my in-depth confession.

I spotted the tall, pillow-lending colleague as he emerged from behind a partition. I tried to catch his eye but he walked politely around me, head lowered, as one might avoid being given a free newspaper. Whether he was silenced by immense guilt or simply busy caring for the very sick was impossible to say.

Eventually, a blue curtain slid aside and Garthene appeared. She sat at the desk across from me, mouthed the words *just wait*, then started typing with her index fingers. I used this time to observe her in her natural habitat, keeping records, saving lives. In fact, I did not observe so much as *gaze upon her*. That made her a little awkward and she ran her hand through her hair. I loved that she was already elegantly silvering. Little glints like when you open the cutlery drawer. Her brown hair was so thick that it disguised the rectangularity of her skull beneath. Garthene's head, at a guess, had the dimensions of a child's shoebox. I adored this about her and looked forward to our retirement when her hair's thinning would reveal further nuances. The fact that I would never guess the exact shape was one of the ways in which our marriage would stay fresh. *To think my younger self thought your skull resembled a child's shoebox when now, I see, it much more closely looks like a deflated plastic football that a child has been sitting on.*

'Stop looking at me like that,' she whispered, without taking her eyes off the screen.

'It's just I love you so much,' I said, and even I could tell how poorly I was able to control the volume of my voice.

She stopped typing.

I rolled my lips inside my mouth.

She found an empty bed on one of the bays. The fresh sheets still showed the grid pattern where they'd been recently folded. In ICU, a newly vacated bed means either someone's got better or died, health or death. I tried to discern which one this was. Health, I decided, based on nothing. Health.

She pulled a curtain around us. 'Don't speak,' she said.

'You're probably wondering what happened to my face.'

'I'm really not.'

'I was punched in it for a very good reason.'

She sprayed my mouth with something that tasted of batteries. 'Just tell me in the morning,' she said, her mouth at my ear.

She put on latex gloves and pulled a metal tray from a cupboard. I watched her pick up a device that resembled a pair of pliers and with the pair of pliers pick up a sterile needle that resembled a fishing hook. She looked like a woman ready to take vengeance on a husband. It was just a shame she did not yet know that I deserved it.

She switched on a bright surgical lamp and hovered it above me. I lay back on the bed, mouth open, enjoying the way the light gave her a halo. As she made the first stitch, I suffered almost no pain, drunk on love and also drunk on alcohol. It was an intimate thing, to feel her at work, tugging tight the dissolvable sutures. I wanted her to sew me up for ever. Close the wound, then close my eyes, ears, and so on, all nine orifices, make me whole again. Instead she sent me home.

I woke on the sofa, which I had elected not to fold out into a bed, as a way to establish a tone of further penitence. I got up and made Garthene a cup of decaffeinated tea the colour she likes it, wet sand. Pushing open the door to our bedroom, I let the hot drink lead. In my face I tried to communicate sombre, sober regret but my mouth was huge and strange and I could not say for sure what shape it made.

I saw straight away that Garthene was in bed with another man and, in that moment, learned something rather disappointing about myself. Though I was holding a cup of freshly boiled tea that I could have easily let fall on to his side of the bed – which is to say my side – thus causing him life-changing burns, I did not do that, because I was not a man of impulse or passion. Instead I put the tea down without spillage because maybe there was a good reason for the muscular man in my bed, which is when I realized it was Lee.

He and my wife had been best friends since secondary school. He used to vet her early boyfriends, warn them that any emotional pain wreaked upon her would come back to them doubled, in the form of normal pain. At university, they had the kind of friendship where they platonically shared a bed during bad break-ups, bad comedowns. When Garthene and I got together she had even warned me that I would need to be comfortable with her receiving regular intimate texts from a buff alpha who was good at football. Still, standing there, I understood that no amount of contextualizing back-story could make this situation feel good.

As my eyes adjusted, I could see that Lee was fully clothed, wearing earplugs and an airline eye mask that had the words *wake me up to eat* printed on it in ten different languages. Garthene was in one of my T-shirts and was, I realized, as her face lit up with blue light, awake and texting.

I went around to her side of the bed. 'Morning,' I said.

'I would have put him on the sofa but you were there.'

'Of course,' I said. 'Totally understand. Did he tell you about last night?'

'He did.'

'It was almost certainly not as bad as that,' I said.

'Okay.' She carried on texting.

On the floor was an open leather weekend bag containing some of Lee's clothes. The uniform of handsome people, fresh white T-shirts and blue jeans. Next to his bag there was the travel cot, the collapsible pram, the pop-up playpen. We were running out of space. I hoped he wouldn't stay long.

'Of course he can stay as long as he wants,' I said.

'Yeah,' she said. 'Might have to.' She stared at her phone.

'Who're you texting?'

'Marie.'

'Oh,' I said.

She mouthed the words: *She says it's over with Lee.*

'But not *over* over?' I said.

I glimpsed the stream of messages on her phone. An intimidating lack of emojis.

'Does he know?' I pointed to the body beside her.

Lee pulled off his eye mask. 'Hey, I'm right here, you fuckers.'

Garthene suggested we go for lunch at one of our favourite restaurants, Old Orient. I knew this could only be in order to deliver bad news. She made sure we got the booth by the noisy mini-waterfall, so that our talk could be private. I ordered what we always order – 'famous Chinese beef' and 'Asian rice' – fully conscious there are thirty-six distinct culinary traditions in mainland China alone. It's the offensive lack of cultural nuance that makes this a place where nobody feels judged.

'Don't worry. She does this every couple of years,' Lee said. 'To keep things fresh.'

'Does what?' Garthene said.

'Breaks up with me. She thinks I'm too secure. She doesn't understand the difference between arrogance and accurate self-worth,' he said, and showed us most of his teeth.

'Tell me you're still drunk,' she said.

'If you need me to be.' He raised his hand and asked the waitress for beer. She said she'd be back in a minute to take his order and, luckily for us, he believed her. Terrible service was part of the reason we loved this place.

'Lee, listen, I think she's genuinely unhappy,' she said.

'Well, it wouldn't work if she didn't pretend to mean it.'

'Wow, okay,' Garthene said, and she took hold of her teacup. There is a scientific study that proves holding hot drinks makes people appear warmer, kinder, more trustworthy. 'Then I need to tell you something.'

'Is it about how you've realized that monogamy is just a way for ugly people to turn their forgettable faces into a matter of principle?' he said. 'No offence to you two.'

I took none. I'd had my small taste of adultery. That nugget of near-betrayal would sustain me till death.

'No,' she said, 'it's about how you make her feel guilty for being insufficiently promiscuous.'

He screwed up his face. 'Please,' he said.

'Marie has only ever slept with you.'

'Come on,' he said. 'I lived with her. I watched her. She went away for weekends. She had *business trips*.'

Garthene put the cup down and slid a hand across the red table-cloth towards him. 'Sweetheart, I think they were actual business trips.'

Marie was co-director of a qualitative research company. Her job involved having deep, personal conversations with ordinary people about, for example, life, death, love and fate, as a way to better understand, for example, dishwasher tablets. She was often conducting intense discussions in airless basements and could Lee be blamed for his assumptions?

He looked around the restaurant, as though there might be some evidence of her infidelity here. He stared at the mini-waterfall, stared through it as though trying to see into the steam room of the upmarket hotel where his wife – he was beginning to realize now – was receiving a completely professional massage.

'So what are you saying?' he said. 'I need to stop fucking around?'

Garthene took hold of his hand. 'I think it might be too late for that.'

We watched his torso shift beneath his shirt as he tried to become a different person.

'All she has to do is ask,' he said. 'I could easily live without.'

Garthene did not contradict him.

The waitress brought the food.

We let silence descend while Lee scanned his memory for any evidence that he was the sort of person who could handle being faithful. Here was a man whose penis had never been told no. He looked down at the bowl of steaming orange beef from which I had selected the softest-looking piece of meat because chewing was difficult for me. It shivered in my chopsticks, resembling a human ear. His eyes were full of panic as he watched me pop it in.

By the time we walked home, Lee was leaning on Garthene. His eyes were squeezed closed, with beads along the joins as though unprofessionally glued. I have always struggled to believe that very good-looking people can achieve authentic melancholy but he was helping me shake off that prejudice.

We neared the office of our estate agent, Daniel Lorrigan. He was the one person on this earth to whom we wished to appear boring and normal. He was a Kiwi with sun-damaged skin and a narrow head, a head we worshipped and despised and always cheerfully waved at past the bottles of Perrier in display fridges. It was within his power to grant or crush our dreams, specifically the horrible maisonette on which we were now gambling all wealth and happiness. He'd told us it was the last family home at its price point within the M25. Once this house was gone we might as well move near my parents in Suffolk, endure the community spirit that fills their numb and empty lives.

I saw my bruised reflection in the floor-to-ceiling windows and, behind me, Lee, wet-faced and putting weight on my visibly pregnant wife. We did not look like valued clients. Daniel waved and smiled from behind his desk, his sunburn picked out by the screen's fluorescence.

I pulled out the sofa bed and made it nice for Lee. We kept spare sheets, pillows and a duvet in a laundry bag at the bottom of my wardrobe. Once we moved into the horrible maisonette, we would buy fancy linens and keep them in a dedicated cupboard, but we were not those people yet.

All that week, Lee slobbed around our flat, calling in sick to work and eating our best granola – the granola so expensive we treat it only as a topping for other, cheaper cereals. It wasn't until Saturday that I managed to get him to go outside. I encouraged him to attend a house party at Dave's. At best, I thought he might see Marie and they would get back together. At second best, I thought he might sleep with a stranger and spend the night at their place. At third best, I thought he might take every drug and forget our address.

But early on Sunday morning, I awoke to something burning. I opened my eyes in the darkness of our bedroom. They say you smell burnt toast just before you have a stroke. And, in retrospect, that might have been preferable. A mini stroke, nothing major, but enough to remind Garthene that she valued my life.

Instead, it was clear by the sound of the pedal bin clanging shut that Lee had come home from the party and was burning actual toast. Garthene stirred at the noise but did not wake. I listened to the bread bin rattle open. We have this very distinctive-sounding bread bin, mid-century chrome, with powerful springs that clatter the lid back. He was going in for a second round.

I sat there, hoping for the sake of our marriage that Lee would successfully complete this entry-level culinary task then pass out for many days on the sofa bed. But a minute passed and a fresh wave of carbonized particulates came under the door. He had ruined the second batch. That takes a special kind of derangement and could only mean his mind was lost to sorrow and drugs.

I hoped Garthene would not wake because, if she did, she would almost certainly get straight out of bed and provide Lee with emotional support. I sat there wishing him unconsciousness. It is amazing how easily depressed people become unsympathetic. I caught myself feeling grateful that Garthene's sinuses were blocked – one of the lesser-known side effects of pregnancy.

Lee opened the cutlery drawer and Garthene's breathing shallowed as he clumsily searched for an implement. Then came a sound. *Shik, shik, shik.* A sharp noise like scratching ice from a windscreen. *Shik, shik, shik.* He was aggressively scraping the burnt bits into the sink. *Shik, shik, shik.* Garthene's body stiffened beside me.

'What's he doing?' she said.

'He's hungry,' I said.

Shik, shik, shik.

In my mind, I saw the black dust falling.

'Has he only just come home?' she said.

'Yes but don't worry. He was probably just having a lot of carefree fun.'

She frowned and checked the time on her phone. There were numerous missed calls, all from Lee. 'Oh God,' she said, and she threw back the duvet.

When I came through, Lee had his head on the kitchen table beside a bottle of brandy with Garthene sitting next to him, rubbing his back, and she had damp splodges and black crumbs on the shoulder of her towelling gown, where he'd been weeping against her.

'You'll feel better after you've had some sleep,' she said.

'I don't want to feel better,' he said.

'How was the party?'

'I'm going out,' he said.

He scraped his chair back and picked up the brandy.

'Hang on,' Garthene said. 'We're coming with you.'

I really didn't want to go with him. I wanted to stay in a dark warm room with my wife.

'That's right, man,' I said. 'We won't let you out of our sight.'

We took him to Hackney Downs. It wasn't a royal or pretty park, just a large square of grass with two tree-lined pathways that crossed in the middle. It was precisely this rudimentary quality that made it feel a safe place to take Lee. No fountains, no swans, nothing that might upset him with beauty or romance.

'What happened?' Garthene asked him.

'Nothing,' he said, and he ran ahead of us.

We watched him jump a low fence into the quiet, woodchipped playground, past a sign that said: *No Unaccompanied Adults*. He got straight on the swings. We approached him from behind, feeling a breeze each time he swung back, the faint scent of tobacco still leaching from him, his shirt inflating. The frame groaned and shivered in the ground as he picked up speed. The heft of an adult male.

'Lee,' Garthene said, 'was Marie at the party?'

'Who's Marie?' he said.

He was now swinging so high that I could see the moulded rubber of the seat's underside each time he came back. He was trying to swing free of his body. The chain went slack at the apex of his swing – a moment of weightlessness – then there was a snapping noise when it grew taut again.

'The thing about her,' Lee said, 'is that she's got *terrible* taste in men.' The pitch of his voice shifted as he swung, making him sound younger then older, slipping in and out of puberty.

'Did you speak to her?' Garthene said. She went around to stand in front of him, stepping over the brandy which was wedged into the woodchip.

'She always likes the good-looking muscly ones,' he yelled, 'and then acts surprised when we turn out to be awful.'

There was the sound of a gate closing and two young girls approached across the playground. They had dresses on, one white, one pink, and they both wore complex sports trainers with bubbles of transparent plastic embedded in the soles. When they looked at me, their expressions let me know my bruised face was very impressive.

'Lee, we should go,' I said.

'No way!' he said.

'I think you should let these nice little girls use the swing,' I said.

'They can use the other one!' he said.

We could see the girls' father approaching across the park, picking up pace as he realized we were not accompanied by a child, except the one *in utero*. I walked around to the front of the swing and gave Lee a serious look. His dismount went badly and he fell hard to his palms and knees. The girl in the white dress walked up to the swing and held the shuddering chain. The girl in the pink had noticed, nestled in the woodchip, the bulbous bottle of brandy which, beneath her gaze, looked absurd and evil. They turned to Lee.

'How old are you?' the white dress said.

He padded around on all fours.

'I'm thirty-three, girls. Pretty young! Super eligible!'

Something about the way their eyes tried to make sense of him was painful. Lee took a swig of the brandy. He suppressed a burp and blew it up towards the sky, as though exhaling cigarette smoke. The gate swung and the girls' father entered the playground, a tall black guy in a wax jacket and loafers without socks. Lee offered him the bottle.

'You shouldn't be here,' he said.

Lee spoke in a baby voice: 'But I'm with my mam-oo and dad-oo.'

The two girls gathered in against their father's legs.

'We're sorry about him,' I said, pulling Lee up.

'My own two parents, ashamed!' he said.

Garthene held the gate open as I guided Lee through. We felt the heat of judgement on the backs of our necks.

At the tennis courts, we stopped to listen to an elderly gentleman practising his first serve, his grunts weirdly erotic. Lee made sex faces in time with each exertion noise.

'Harder,' he told the man, in a breathy voice.

Once we got him out of the park, he walked a few steps ahead of us, trying the handles of all the car doors.

'So, did you speak to Marie?'

'No. Apparently she wanted to have a *quiet one* at home. On a Saturday night,' he said, then he tapped his index finger against his chin as though deep in thought. 'I've known her a long time and I must say that sounds highly suspicious.'

Outside the vegan café, he found a small Peugeot's passenger side door that did open and he roared with laughter and got in, his knees pressed against the glovebox. We dragged him out on to the pavement and shut the door behind him.

'Haven't you two got better things to do?' he said.

Garthene told him we didn't then she poured the brandy down a drain.

We walked towards the Church of the Mountain of Healing Faith where the street was busy with people in suits and ornate robes, more getting out of family vehicles, checking for cyclists as they opened their doors. We became separated from Lee as we weaved through and then he started to run. We should have reacted more quickly. We watched him go straight past the door to our building and turn down Glenarm Road.

'Lee!' I yelled.

Garthene stopped. She closed her eyes.

'Where's he going?' I said.

'He still has the keys to Marie's flat.'

We heard his footsteps getting quieter.

While Garthene got out her phone and called Marie, I asked my body to run.

Marie lived on a small, gated development, an oval of neat grass around which fifteen detached buildings were arranged in a three-quarter circle. The spear-topped gates were manned twenty-four hours a day. We dared not ask Marie about her annual service charge. People who own their own homes have to find something to waste their money on.

Our favourite guard was Yuku, and as I rounded the corner at pace, I could see Lee hugging him around the waist, lifting him off the floor. Yuku was the son of a Gurkha and, sometimes, at Marie and Lee's parties, when all of our friends revealed themselves as incredibly boring, I liked to come down and talk to him about his family history and his brief, unbeaten mixed martial arts career, about the inflated bodies of men three times his size going gorgeously limp as he crushed their carotid artery. Lee put Yuku down and went through the gate. Yuku was still chuckling when I got there, out of breath.

'Ray, my friend, who ruined your face?'

'Don't worry, Yuku,' I said. 'I totally deserved it.'

He liked that and he let me pass.

I followed the scuff marks on the lawn to Marie's house. Lee was already inside but had left the front door open, indicating that some small sober part of him wanted me to restrain his worst instincts. I went inside. On the dining table, I saw there were two empty glasses, two dirty plates, and a half-finished bottle of real-cork wine with both its front and back labels peeled off and shredded, the scraps arranged in the table's centre as a cruel, conspicuous shrine to sexual tension.

I stepped quietly up the stairs and down the corridor towards the open door of Marie's bedroom. That's where I saw Lee. He was army-crawling on his stomach, disappearing out of sight around the end of the bed. Marie was on the near side, facing me, the sheet pulled to her neck, her sleeping expression so relaxed as to be unfamiliar, hair tucked like a chinstrap. Her phone was vibrating silently on her bedside table, presumably Garthene, the handset shuffling towards the edge. I stopped just outside the room, and that's when I saw a large man sleeping beside Marie with one hand behind his head. His armpit hair was cutely but naturalistically parted. He either had a full-body tan or a Mediterranean bloodline. The phone stopped twitching for a few seconds then started again until the handset hung, half on the table, half off. Perhaps it would have been better if I'd let it clatter loudly on the floorboards and wake everyone so that Lee and this new man could speak in the basic language of physical violence, make a scene on the lawn, have Yuku render them both unconscious. Instead I stepped forward and caught the phone as it fell.

Now I was inside the room. Light was coming in through the blinds and I could see Lee at the end of the bed, searching the pockets of the man's jeans, the steel-capped tip of a thick leather belt lolling schlongishly. Lee found what he wanted, then there was a clunking sound – belt buckle on floorboard – and the man in the bed rolled on his side towards me. To see him change position was to come to terms with his musculature. It was actually offensive to me that Marie had not lowered her standards. Did it never cross her mind to get with ugly or weak men? He was probably not a model but only because he had another, more fulfilling career, as a researcher into sea pollutants, or a director of a halfway house. He snored in a tremulous way that sounded like someone carefully peeling masking tape off a valuable package. His clean white shirt was crumpled on the desk. Good-looking people and their clean white clothes. Splayed on the floor were Marie's velvety leggings, inside out, and it was hard not to visualize the rabidity of their undressing. Not that they were even drunk. They had not finished one bottle. Why dilute perfection? And this all *well* within the M25. Zone Two. The marital bed.

Lee opened the man's wallet, pulled out a driving licence and took a photo of it with his phone. I tried to disapprove with my eyes but a part of me, a large part, wanted him to enjoy himself. He lifted the bottom of the bed sheet, made a show of peering in, then did a 'this big' action with his hands out wide. I was smiling now. Lee shuffled around to the bed's far side and I saw his head dip as he noticed something on the floor. There was a sticky sound. Lee crawled back with a condom, neatly tied off as you would a balloon, hanging limp in his teeth.

*

When we got him back to the flat, he pinned the condom to our cork board so that we would never forgive or forget. It was impossible to ignore the unseemly weight that hung in the reservoir teat.

'Five hundred million hardbodies frying in spermicide,' Lee said.

Garthene gave him warm water in a dimpled pint tankard, allowing him to enjoy the illusion of heavy drinking while getting hydrated.

'It's bedtime,' she said.

'Maybe for you,' he said.

He pulled out his phone, found the photo of the driving licence and read out the man's name: 'Ladies and gentlemen, I give you William Colin Garfitt. Born in 1974. Lives on Well Street.'

In the photo, William was staring directly out, slight smile at his lips, tremendous jawline casting a shadow on his neck. Below that, there was an intimidating fluidity to his signature.

Lee opened the laptop at the dining table and, without pause, searched for *William Garfitt*.

'Oh God,' he said. 'No social media, and you know what that means.' Lee shook his head in horror. 'Too busy living his worthwhile life.'

As Lee carried on searching, I looked to Garthene for guidance. Was this a situation where we should be providing a strong moral framework or was it best to let Lee make his own mistakes? She didn't seem to know.

'Oh, I've found his job,' Lee said. 'He works for, wait for it, Thames Water.' Lee roared with laughter. 'Infrastructure!'

Neither Garthene nor I were sure whether this was funny or reprehensible.

Lee clicked Play on a video titled 'Tour of the Walthamstow Reservoirs'. A fourth voice entered the room.

'*Hey, guys, my name's Will and I'm going to show you round the reservoirs today. Welcome to my office!*'

'Nice,' Lee said. 'Because it's not an office.'

We watched William's broad shoulders shift beneath his polo shirt as he walked backwards between trees.

'*All sorts of wildlife thrive here. Trout, bass and barbel; herons, geese and moorhens. Our moorhens winter in Morocco. It's all right for some!*'

'Ha ha ha ha ha, great joke,' Lee said.

Garthene and I looked at each other.

'*Meanwhile, we work hard to keep the reservoir healthy, from monitoring algal blooms through to mechanically oxygenating the water.*'

Behind William, the water in the reservoir blinked. Lee's eyes widened.

'We should probably stop stalking this man now,' I said, and I looked at Garthene.

'Ray's right,' she said.

We were united. What a feeling. We were just like real parents with our consistent ethical boundaries.

Lee was not listening.

'*If you live in East London – from every bath you take to every cup of tea you drink – it all starts life right here. Though of course we recommend you take showers, not baths!*'

It was obvious from William's unselfconscious laughter that this man loved his job, was proud to have a measurable impact on everyday lives. And though Lee had a good job too, at a creative agency called Kindness, there was no competing with someone who worked in the proximity of trees. Furthermore, Lee's office was ostentatiously fun – with ping-pong and hammocks on the roof terrace – a work environment so clearly meant to free the imagination that it constantly reminded him that, as website manager, his particular role was mundane and mechanistic, perhaps second only to the accounts team, with whom he shared dark looks of joyless detachment across the stand-up meetings.

'*Now follow me as we meet some of the fascinating wildlife —*'

I closed the laptop, locking William Garfitt back in his box.

Garthene put a hand on Lee's shoulder. 'You're better than this,' she said.

He turned in his seat to look at her. 'I really don't think I am,' he said.

We finally put Lee to bed with the curtains drawn, but they let the light in, so I strung up a blanket as a blackout, knotted its corners to the rail. He slept right through into the night and did not rise on Monday. This happens to some patients in hospital too. They call it sundowning, when the body clock drifts. Since Garthene was starting a run of night shifts, she and he became synchronized. I was the odd one out, still committed to the hours of daylight.

On Tuesday afternoon — while they both slept — I had time to dwell on my situation. I wondered if Garthene was ever going to make the time to get angry with me about what happened at the party. I didn't like the idea that she was storing up her rage, letting it pickle. Or worse, that I might have been pre-punished but did not know about it. That my incident with Marie was nothing when compared to what she had already done with a tall, pillow-generous nurse on a gurney. Or even that Garthene was simply not that bothered. Which was perhaps the most frightening of all.

On Wednesday morning, I woke to find them having dinner together in the still-darkened kitchen-lounge which was now, also, Lee's bedroom. He raised his glass of beer to me as I came out in my dressing gown.

'Evening!' he said.

At his feet there was a row of empty cans and on top of the table was his laptop, open and glowing.

'Morning,' I said.

Garthene smiled, apologetically. They were eating supermarket sushi with their hands. I made myself a cup of tea, tried to ignore the condom on the cork board by the kettle, how the sperm had cooked down to a single translucent pearl.

'You feeling any better, Lee?' I said.

'Much,' he said.

'Have you been awake all night?'

He squeezed some wasabi paste on to his index finger and rubbed it into his rear gums.

'What have you been doing?' I said.

'Catching up on admin!' He slapped his laptop shut.

The swing in his voice was unsettling.

While I cleared away the sushi boxes and the little plastic soy sauce fish, they brushed their teeth. Lee scrubbed his tongue until he retched. Then he did it again. By the third time it was clear he was enjoying it.

Once he was in bed, I went into our room to speak to Garthene. I shut the door and, with my hand outstretched, felt for the edge of the bed and sat beside her.

'What's he been doing?'

'I'm not sure. He's on his computer a lot,' she said.

'I know you're talking about me,' Lee yelled from the lounge. 'I'm totally fine and happy!'

We lowered our voices.

'I feel like we never get the chance to really speak to each other.'

'I know,' Garthene said. 'I'm sorry. I'm just so tired.'

'How was work?'

'Long.'

'I hope you had a sleep break?'

'Yes.'

'That's good,' I said. 'Borrow any nice pillows?'

I was trying to find a way to have fun with the idea of infidelity, making it something we could laugh about, but she didn't seem to understand, or didn't want to.

'Sorry,' she said, 'what does that mean?'

'When I came to the hospital, I saw that a tall, handsome colleague of yours had lent you his pillow,' I said, letting the tone of my voice indicate light-heartedness. 'And I can only imagine what you and Mr Thoughtful get up to while your patients are sedated.'

It's hard to make her laugh when she's tired.

I leaned forward and, navigating by her breath alone, kissed what felt like her eyelid in the gloom.

Back in the dark kitchen-lounge-bedroom, I sat at the dining table. There was nothing for it but to repress all worries and focus on work.

I opened my laptop and typed in the light from my screen, tapping the keys quietly, doing my best to ignore Lee's presence on the sofa bed. He didn't snore exactly but his open-mouthed breathing was tangible, musky and warm, like the exhaust vent of a vacuum cleaner. I tried to concentrate. I reminded myself that I was going to be a father soon and that was expensive. Also, Techtracker.co.uk only paid ten pence a word. In the old days, I enjoyed sneaking a sentence of exclusively two- and three-letter words into an article as a way to wreak utterly futile vengeance on my employers. *Do buy it if – big if – the men at LG can fix the bug in the Blu-ray.* That sentence works out at almost four pence a letter, suckers. But at some point you have to put away tiny rebellions and just get on with your worthless job.

As I tried to write a three-hundred-worder about how smart thermostats now link to smart watches that track your body temperature, thus making your home an extension of your own flesh, the smell in my actual room became richer, more intimate. My eyes adjusted to the dark and I noticed the pile of baby objects beside the sofa. A bouncer, a basket, a sheepskin and a handful of toys so ugly they seemed specifically designed to appal my sense of aesthetics. I imagined Lee's downcast gases seeping into it all, the hypoallergenic fabrics marinating in his adult sorrow, the Octoplush's eight cheerful melodies suddenly bluesy and minor. Consider the stink of a grown man's melancholy through a newborn's gleaming nostrils. I had this feeling that Lee would live on our sofa for ever, that our child would call him Uncle and find his lifestyle inspirational.

I received a message from our estate agent, Dan. He rarely brought us happiness. *Hey, dude, I'll need your final bid by 5pm today. It's between you and the cash buyers now. If you want a last look, let me know. I'll be there this afternoon. D xx*

I got double kisses from our agent. We'd been through so much.

Garthene and I had agreed that we could not afford to raise our offer. So it was clear we would now lose the horrible maisonette and go on renting until death, needing a flatmate, needing Lee to sleep on our sofa, to fill our lives with his sad smells and functional alcoholism and necessary contribution to the bills.

I closed my laptop and went outside, into the daylight and the fresher air of Clapton's most congested arterial thoroughfare. Many journalists swear a brisk walk helps them come up with irresistible feature ideas. I walked north, thinking absolutely nothing. By the pond I examined the tall, terraced Georgian houses. Most of them had five or more buzzers for each front door, which was acceptable, but a few of them had just a single doorbell or, in the case of number 8, which was a huge detached house with wide gates and a gravelled loop of driveway, a lone knocker in the shape of a human hand. Nobody deserved that much space in London. I fundamentally hated these people while simultaneously wanting to be them.

Throughout our twenties, it had been embedded in our world view that to even talk about property was death itself – the clue was the word *mortgage*, 'death pledge' in French. Then we hit our thirties, Garthene got pregnant and we started going to viewings. Though we tried to maintain a moral superiority, soon we found ourselves rapping our knuckles against partition walls and saying, without irony, *We could knock this through*.

I continued north, watching the houses get smaller, meaner, cheaper. A young boy saw my colourful face and stopped kicking his ball. There was pleasure in being the scariest person in the street. I walked alongside the Lea, one of the country's most polluted and slow-moving rivers, full of stringy weeds that stretched out beneath the surface like the hair of drowned children. Children who had drowned, I decided, because they'd grown up in rented top-floor flats with no outside space, faux-uncles watching pornography in their play zone during daylight hours, and so they'd ended up down here by the river, depressed, and look, now they were dead.

I arrived at our former future home, the horrible maisonette, one among many in a joyless four-storey block. Though it was unquestionably ugly, it was impossible not to love the private front garden and braced wooden gate. The gate was wholesome. I couldn't help but imagine our child, who we loved, coming in from school through it. Our child, who we loved, opening it to receive their charmingly disreputable friends.

I sat down on a bench by the river and watched birds circling the wetland centre. They looked like seagulls, but probably that was just my ignorance and they were something more profound.

We had never visited the wetland centre but were working hard at wanting to. The front gate. The river. The swans. The marshes were the third biggest park in London. I closed my eyes and thought of everything we were about to lose.

After some time I heard a voice: 'And I'm sure you two know this is pretty much the last family home at this price point anywhere within the M25.'

I opened my eyes. I heard the sound of a gate clinking gently shut.

I waited a moment before turning around. In the residents' car park I saw Dan's Volkswagen e-Golf, a car he charges from a three-pin domestic socket. Next to it was a Qashqai. I felt something shift inside me and two words bubble to the surface: *cash buyers*. It just wasn't fair for a young family like us to have to compete with these people. Though I didn't have my baby yet, I already had my righteousness. I stood up, walked to the front gate. The buyers were out of sight but I could see Dan, in short sleeves, leaning against the pale kitchen counter which needed updating.

I went around to the back of the block, the loose paving stones clunking behind our former future neighbours' homes, their tropical pot plants and bikes with missing wheels and sad little zones of gravel. I slowed as I reached number 5 and peered into the empty lounge. The buyers were presumably upstairs, and I knew Dan would not see me. He had an Antipodean no-pressure style and would hang back in the kitchen, checking his phone. The walls in the lounge were two-tone: navy at the bottom and baby blue above. The thin municipal-looking carpet was speckled with dots, possibly slug pellets, and had a scald mark from a clothes iron. During our viewing, I had bent down and touched where the burn had blackened the carpet to hard plastic. We had *enjoyed* the blemish, Garthene and I, had imagined peeling back the carpet to reveal the floorboards beneath. Just the thought of *discovering* floorboards. Bourgeois archaeology. And even if it was concrete under there, no problem. We would polish it.

As I looked into the lounge I saw the hands of the cash buyers on the banisters as they came slowly downstairs. The word *banister* filled me with an ache I could not name. I had never lived across two floors in London. Newel post, I thought, with longing, as they reached the bottom step. They were our age and looked like us, she in a denim dungaree dress and basketball high-tops, he in a light pink shirt and deck shoes. The woman made a two-handed signal, something like a breaststroke, that seemed to indicate knocking a wall through. That made the decision for me.

I put up my hood and stepped close to the window, my bruised face at the glass. The sun stretched my shadow ghoulishly across the room. I raised my right hand and pressed it softly, fingers bent, against the glass. That was damn scary. Perhaps I had seen it in films.

The woman's stomach entered the lounge. Let me be the first to say I did not set out to terrify a woman in her third trimester, though her life was repulsively comfortable. Then came the rest of her. She looked up, saw me, yelled, just once but loud – 'oh!' – like a tennis umpire, then put one hand to her stomach and the other to the panel of the door. Her husband's head appeared and his eyes widened as they met mine. Given that I was presenting no immediate threat, I was impressed by his willingness to act. His face retreated and a moment later I watched the back-door handle turn frantically but it was double-locked. A moment later I saw him run back down the corridor. He was ready to defend his wife, unborn child and future community. These were the kinds of people you want as neighbours.

I turned and ran south down the street, into Millfields Park, towards the wildflower meadow. The topless drunks on the outdoor gymnasium equipment raised their cans as I passed. At the basket-ball courts, I glanced back and saw the man, the father-to-be, following at full pelt. That his shirt stayed tucked in as he ran was intimidating. He had a prospective new dad's insane motivation. Performance-enhancing emotions. I wanted to tell him I empathized completely with his need to perform elaborate heroics. *We are brothers*, I wanted to say, but he could really run – was conceivably an athlete – and so I had to focus on pumping my arms and legs.

I kept going until the homes became unaffordable again. It was a hot day and my scalp bloomed with sweat. It was reassuring to know that, at this speed, the horrible maisonette was not more than nine minutes from the amenities of Lower Clapton. I stopped out-side the leisure centre, where my heavy breathing had an acceptable context. I looked behind me. He was gone. At some point, the man's desire to chase me through the streets had been overcome by the realization that he had left his pregnant wife alone in an ungentrified neighbourhood, a neighbourhood too full of unstable, swollen-faced men for them ever to live there. I stood on the pavement, the salt of my sweat stinging my wound. This was my city, my pain. I was the winner. *We* had won. Our child would get the happiness.

I sat in the dark, uncle-scented lounge, waiting for Garthene to wake up so I could tell her the good news. I opened one of Lee's beers to celebrate. I was on to my third by the time our bedroom door opened and Garthene shuffled out in her dressing gown, walk-ing with the light from her phone.

'I just got a message from Dan,' she said.

She showed me the screen.

Bad news, guys. Predictably, the sellers have gone with the cash. But I've got a killer two-bed in East Ham I really want to show you (just a smidge over budget). We march on. xx

The phone went dark. We were lit only by the twitching of the Wi-Fi router. I could not see her expression. We listened to Lee's juddering breath, pumping the room full of hopelessness.

I got up, went to the window. We needed to get him out. I pulled down the blackout blanket and watched the objects of the small rented room materialize: table, chairs, kettle, toaster, bouncer, basket, condom on a cork board, two empty cans beneath my seat, pregnant wife's face of only moderate disappointment, sad man rolling away from the light.

Even at midday, with the windows all open, lights on, and me typing as loudly as I could, jabbing my index finger at each key in turn, I was unable to drive Lee out of bed, let alone our lives. I read aloud a study that shows that if one of your colleagues even *tells* you they are hungover it reduces *your* work rate as much as theirs. He had his earplugs in. After that, I did try working in the nearby coffee shop, but the glimpses of other people's laptop screens – running Final Draft or Final Cut – all these thirty-somethings who still hadn't given up their dreams, it was disgusting. So I came back home, where at least I didn't have to buy a coffee in order to procrastinate. I spent my time trying to think of ways to get rid of Lee. Might I buy him a gym membership? Or help him write a misleading dating profile? Or take him to the GP for beta blockers? Finally I settled on palming him off on our other friends. That was the whole point of friends: to replace the family, welfare state and mental-health services. I sent around a group message, suggesting a weekday picnic in Lee's honour. I explained how he was finding life hard and it is at times like this that real friends come together to show how much we care and how many spare rooms we have.

'Everyone wants to see you, pal,' I said, sitting on the end of Lee's bed, resting my hand on his shin through the duvet.

His eyes scrunched and then opened a fraction. It was now 5 p.m, another work day wasted.

'Have you invited Marie?' he said.

I replied in my soothing voice: 'No. But I will if you want me to.'

He sat up and uncorked his head, twisting out the earplugs. 'Yes, I think I'm ready,' he said, and though he did not seem ready – speaking, as he was, from a bed in which I could see gross little tufts of claggy toilet paper protuding from where he had wedged them under the mattress – I decided to believe him.

It was true that on the day of the picnic he started drinking at lunchtime but he did so quietly, politely opening a can beneath the table, tapping his fingernail against the lid to ease fizz before opening. *Tck tck tck*. His nerves settled, we stepped outside. The sun split the high street in two, one pavement in darkness, one in light, and we chose the light. It never actually rains in London. The only people who think that don't live here. As we crossed over into the park through the smell of aggressive barbecuing, he did a little hop in his walk to set a carefree tone. I'd returned him to the world.

We saw them, our friends, on a tartan blanket out by the treeline, half in shade, half not. It was a testament to the sheer, preposterous luxuriousness of our lives that a Monday afternoon picnic was so well attended. I was impressed to see Marie there already, sitting in a checked dress with her legs tucked underneath her.

She stood up when she saw him. It was clear that she did not know if a hug was appropriate or did not feel that she was in a position to initiate it. Beside her, the twins were trying to walk, tumbling over adorably, laughing as they stacked it – recasting failure as a kind of joy – and this created the perfect atmosphere. Lee bravely opened his arms and went forward. Marie raised herself up on her toes to allow clean contact. We all watched them perform their maturity. The hug lasted longer than a mere greeting but, equally, did not overextend into neediness or patronizing sympathy.

Once Marie and Lee finished hugging, Dave clapped and we all went around, kissing one another. I don't know when we'd started kissing on both cheeks as a greeting but probably London was to blame and if, at first, there'd been a little sarcasm in it – we were making fun of theatre people – that was gone now and we were just those people.

I knelt down on the grass to take in the babies, Lydia and Lucy, both only a quarter black but those quarters meant a lot to us. With their mother Kamara's half on top of that plus Garthene's Keralan grandmother that was one and a quarter in total. More than one of my friends. It felt good. I kissed the twins' heads, then flopped down on the grass.

Marie and Lee took to opposite corners of the blanket, Dave Finlay between them, to mediate. Dave had tidied his beard and moustache, I noticed. There was a clear border between neck growth and chest hair, his lips cutely framed.

Michael was helping the twins practise walking on the short grass. Both girls were wearing their Royal Guardsman sleepsuits with the gold epaulettes. Michael and Kamara had signed them up to an agency, Smaller Models, and their first gig had been for a website called TheRoyalCollection.com. Though the clothes were given to them as freebies, it was still necessary to think less of Michael and Kamara for dressing their children in the apparatus of monarchy. It was easy to feel judgemental when Garthene and I knew, instinctively, genetically, modelling would not be an option for our child.

Michael and I watched Lydia holding a Rattle-Me sceptre. He pointed to the left breast of his daughter's sleepsuit, the Velcro medals: 'She fought in both world wars and was awarded the Victoria Cross,' he said.

'Brave little soldier,' I said.

We watched Lydia struggle to take a step.

'Lost the use of her lower limbs though,' Michael said. 'Shrapnel severed the spine.'

I chuckled. He was smart to make a joke out of it.

Lydia took two quick steps then stood there, arms outstretched for balance.

'For our tomorrow, she gave her today,' Michael said.

I smiled but didn't laugh. Lydia took another step then sat down. That was the end of Michael's skit. He reached into his rucksack and pulled out a bottle in a metallic cooling sleeve. The wine had a crimped metal cap, like a beer, which Michael removed using a trick with his wedding ring. I'd never seen a wine bottle with a beer-style cap before, and I knew that it probably marked the relaxed house style of a young winemaker well beyond my budget.

'Here, have some English champagne,' Michael said, 'overpriced and disgusting.'

It did taste disgusting but in that particular, wealthy way that made me feel it was a personal failing rather than any problem with the drink.

'It's unfiltered,' Michael said, then he lay back on his elbows and watched the sky. There was something unusually relaxed about him that I didn't like. He was wearing a blue carpenter's shirt, identical to one I owned, except his top button was sewn on with red thread, while the rest used black, and that top button had five holes so the red thread illustrated a tiny, evil pentagram. It was one of those near-imperceptible details designed to let me know that, although at first glance our shirts were identical, his was funda-mentally superior.

'Michael,' I said, 'how much do the twins make as models?'

'Not much,' he said, without looking me in the eye.

'Right. That's what rich people say.'

'Ha ha,' Michael said, and he closed his eyes.

'But seriously,' I said. 'How much?'

'Do you really want to know?'

'Now I'm terrified,' I said.

'It's not that bad. They get around ninety an hour for a shoot, then it's a lump sum – *five figs* – if they get used in a big campaign.' He said *five figs* in a jokey voice, but the jokey voice could not save him from having said *five figs*.

Michael smiled and drank his champagne. I felt a momentary urge to drag him into the middle of the park and crush his carotid artery. I transposed that desire into raising my plastic glass and saying: 'To you, to your beautiful daughters.'

For the next half hour, the conversation stayed as light and vacuous as the ribbons of bubbles in the humiliating wine and we clapped the twins whenever they managed to string a few piddling steps together.

'Tell them about your new boyfriend,' Kamara said and, at first, I thought she was talking to Marie, then realized she was talking to Dave. It was important never to be shocked when a friend's sexuality took a swerve.

'Oh, boys now, is it?' I said.

'It's always been boys,' Dave said.

'Always since when?'

'Since I was a zygote,' he said.

'Oh, sure.'

Had he always been gay? Or had he switched? Perhaps it was one of those situations where no one had wanted to tell me, on account of how excited I would be. I lay back on the grass, feeling the weight of my body. I had never changed sexuality, not once. Some of us are locked into our straightness, no key to the closet.

'Tell us his name,' Michael said.

'Alan,' he said. 'But spelt double el ee en, which I think makes all the difference.'

He was right. Allen. It changed everything.

'And he's fit as Christ,' Kamara said, bouncing a daughter in her arms.

'True,' Dave said. 'I'm punching way above my weight.'

I turned away to look at the sun, let my corneas burn. It felt good to have the handsome, hopeful faces of my friends replaced by a blank white dot, a hole punched where their smiles might be.

'That's great, Dave,' Lee said, speaking calmly to the sky, where a helicopter was hovering. 'And how about you, Marie? What's new in your world?' It could have been a strange, artificial turn in the conversation, but the tone of his voice was in keeping with the frothy atmosphere.

I felt then that Lee would soon be reunited with Marie in the house that she owns and that Michael and Kamara's one-year-old twins would earn enough through modelling to pay the deposit on a garden flat and that Dave and Allen would be rich in the way gay couples always are, all my friends accelerating into a higher grade of happiness, leaving me and Garthene to our moderate existence, manageable contentment, a child we work hard to love in a room we do not own.

Marie pulled an olive stone from between her lips and flicked it high towards the cricket square. 'Nothing much,' she said. 'Work. How's life on Lower Clapton Road?'

'Yeah, good. Regressing into childhood, with Ray and Garthene my primary caregivers,' Lee said and he laughed.

I looked at Marie, except there was a giant cigarette burn where her face should be.

'We're ever so proud,' I said.

'The other day we all went to the playground just behind those trees,' Lee said.

'He makes us feel young again,' I said. 'We love each other by loving him.'

They didn't hear my bitterness. Really happy people don't pick up on tone. Lee was smiling in my peripheral vision so I could not help but see it, his teeth all his own.

'I was on the swings and I swung and swung and swung,' Lee said, his voice musical now, slightly overdone, 'until I was so dizzy I could hardly see or think.'

'He did,' I said. 'He didn't want to stop. He wouldn't even let these two cute little girls have a go.'

'Why should they get special treatment?' he said. 'We're only as old as we feel and I feel pre-school.'

Marie laughed, though it wasn't very funny.

Lee waited for quiet before carrying on, now speaking more slowly. 'And afterwards I was *so* confused that I just *did not know* where I was. So much so that I ended up going home to the wrong house.'

Only at that point did I realize he was telling the story about breaking into Marie's flat. This meant Lee was in fact not totally healthy and happy. Marie didn't know what was coming, so she just smiled and picked up an anchovy from its oil, hung it from her fingers then, timing the moment between drips, craned it into her mouth.

'Just muscle memory, I guess,' Lee said. 'But I ended up at Longford Close. Yuku let me through.'

She chewed steadily then swallowed. She was not panicking yet.

'That's weird,' she said. 'When was this?'

I got up on my elbow.

'It was like I'd completely forgotten I didn't live with you any more,' Lee said, and he laughed. 'And I still have a key to your place, so I was all like,' he cupped one hand around his mouth, calling up to the sky, above the noise of the helicopters – two of them now – slicing the air, '*ho-ney, I'm home.*'

I was not the most broken person at the picnic. Lee was way more broken than me.

'When did this happen?' Marie said.

All other conversations subsided as her voice tightened. One of the twins took six quick consecutive steps then tumbled gorgeously but nobody applauded.

Lee looked to me. 'This was *when*, Ray? A week ago? It was a Sunday morning maybe? I think so, yes, Sunday, just before breakfast.'

Marie's jaw tensed and there was a glimpse of the spoked pattern along which her mouth would one day wrinkle.

'You were out cold, Marie,' Lee said. 'Sparko. Little rouge on your lips from that mid-price wine.'

'You shouldn't have done that,' she said.

'It was an accident,' he said, and he held up his hands as though at gunpoint. 'And you were in bed with this absolute dreamboat. It actually made me feel better to see how good-looking William was.'

Marie turned to look directly at the sun. Lee dug a pitta strip into the mackerel pâté, reinforced it with his finger for a more powerful scoop, then ate it in one.

Marie breathed out slowly. 'Ahhh,' she said, relieved, as though everything up to that point, all the good-naturedness, had been a huge effort. '*Fuck* you.' The words rang loud and true.

Lee made a show of reaching over and covering little Lydia's ears, though Michael and Kamara felt bad words were a part of life and it would only give them a special power, the bad words, if they were forbidden.

'I'm honestly glad he's hot and I'm glad because he seems a decent guy, your William,' Lee said. 'He could be *the one*.'

'Well,' Dave said, dusting his hands together, 'I think we should call time on this conversation. Who wants to play pétanque?'

'I'll play,' Lee said.

Marie's left hand was gripping the grass, tufts of it poking between her knuckles. 'How do you know his name?' she said.

'What, William's name? The name William? Bill? Bill Garfitt? Billy G?'

Dave stood up. 'Let's play over there,' he said, pointing to the far side of the park, near where a police van was throwing pretty blue and white lights among the trees.

'Did you know about this, Ray?' Marie said.

I looked down at the tartan blanket. I was a coward.

'Every time I run myself a bath,' Lee said, his voice loud now, 'I take a little moment to give thanks for the hard work of William . . . Colin . . . Garfitt.' He said the full name slowly, relished every syllable. 'And, of course, the rest of the team at Thames Water.'

There was a pause. Lee saw something in Marie's face, then spoke in a tuneful way: 'Hasn't he, hasn't William told you he works for Thames Water? That he has ten years' experience in the water industry? Hasn't he offered to give you a tour of the reservoirs?'

Marie necked her plastic glass of wine in one clean gulp. Her lips were shiny.

'No,' she said, 'I guess we've been too busy having all this life-changing sex.'

'Of course,' Lee said, and he clicked his fingers and pointed at her as though she had just come up with a great idea. 'He must be tremendous in bed.'

'Oh, he is,' Marie said. 'He has literally *no* insecurities. It's terrifying, actually.'

'Well, you can't look like him and not be invincible,' Lee said.

'Absolutely,' Marie said. 'He is in complete control of his orgasm. It is a matter of as and when.'

Lee roared with laughter. The sound travelled out across the park. A couple who were power-walking along the path looked over. They were either power-walking or terribly frightened. I can never tell the difference.

By the far trees, there were now four male civilians facing the side of the police van, their legs spread, a hint of music video choreography. An officer, using both hands, squeezed one man's left leg from ankle to thigh. It was a surprise to note how skinny the man was beneath his jeans, skinny enough that it was necessary to retrospectively downgrade him to boy.

'They don't stop and search me, do they?' Michael said, standing on the cricket square with a daughter in one arm. He was trying to change the subject. 'Officer, officer,' he said, raising his free hand to the police as though signalling for a waiter, 'I'm an Anglo-Saxon father of twins with cocaine in my shirt pocket.'

'Officer, officer, please arrest this man for bad satire,' Kamara said, jiggling the other daughter.

'I confess,' Michael said. 'I confess only to highlighting institutionalized prejudice. And anyway, this coke is so heavily cut it's basically legal.'

Marie and Lee were staring at each other.

A Welsh male voice choir started in Dave's pocket. As he pulled out his phone – which had a thick and sticky rubber casing for people who lead extreme lives – it brought with it the contents of his right pocket: a two-euro coin and a small vial of a colourless liquid, presumably sex drugs. All my happy friends were secretly hollow. That was a calming thought.

'Father dearest, how can I help you?' Dave said, answering the call and stepping away from the blanket.

'You should ask William about me, Marie,' Lee said. 'Though, of course, he won't know me as boring old Lee. To him I am,' Lee spoke in a silky voice and flicked imaginary hair from his shoulder, '*Elnaz Mahroo*.'

'You can stop this now,' Marie said.

'I'm serious,' he said. 'Elnaz is my alter ego. I'm a Persian human rights lawyer with a hard body and strong ethics and a passion for late-night photo sharing.' He got out his phone, tapped it a few times, then showed everyone a picture of a very attractive woman with flawless skin, wearing a white shirt, her high ponytail flowing like freshly struck oil. 'William and I first got to know each other on LinkedIn. But it's a professional network, so when we wanted to get personal we shifted the whole thing to Gchat.'

'I'm going,' Marie said.

'Wait,' Lee said. 'Your man is really talented. I presume he's told you about his artistic side?'

She started putting her things into a black tote bag.

'The man's a *geni*us,' Lee said, and he swiped his phone a few times, then said: 'Hang on, let me find his best work,' and held it up to her.

She squinted briefly at the screen. 'I don't know what that is.'

Across the field, two more police vans arrived.

Dave, on his phone, turned away from us, saying: 'Oh shit . . . *right now?*'

'Try this one,' Lee said, and he flicked the screen onwards. 'I think that is genuinely artistic. His penis is not even the dominant feature of the photo.'

Marie glanced at the phone, then looked down, closed her eyes.

'He's very innovative within the genre.' Lee kept the sing-song tone in his voice.

There were more riot vans – five in total – coming along the north side of the park, sirens on, lights flashing, as though they had been asked to provide staging for Lee's cruelty.

Dave put his finger to his ear. '*What?* That's awful.'

'And look at this one,' Lee said, holding his phone up so we could all see the self-taken picture of a gently left-curving penis bathed in warm light, a toned body stretched out on scrubby grass, his head out of shot. 'It's clear golden hour gives William a massive rod-on. A true artist.'

This was all very well executed. I now knew what Lee had been doing, late at night, in the darkness of our lounge.

Marie stood up, but her balance was out so she keeled a little and took a compensatory step back, crushed a paper plate with her heel, baba ganoush oozing from the complex grooves of her running shoe's sole.

'Whoopsy,' Lee said.

Marie walked away to scuff her foot on thicker grass.

'No way, no way, no way,' Dave said. 'Those poor people.'

I had tuned out the sound of the helicopters. Like the way you can not notice a kettle come to the boil. There were now three of them hovering beyond the estate. Three phones on the blanket, including mine, were receiving calls. They had been ringing for some time. All the calls came from the same person: *Mum*. I hadn't spoken to mine in weeks.

Lee kept on talking, raising his voice, speaking high and clear above the noise. 'I sent him some pictures of me to get the ball rolling, but nothing prepared me for the quality of his composition, the play of light, sense of movement, a strong organizing principle that goes well beyond the rule of thirds into something more instinctive. I hesitate to say Cartier-Bresson, but he's certainly there as a presiding spirit and . . .'

Marie hid her face behind her hands. Her breathing changed.

'Aw diddums,' Lee said.

'Everyone,' Dave said. 'We need to get inside. There's something happening on the high street.'

'What kind of thing?'

'It's on the news. There're buses on fire and my dad says it's madness, and it's spreading.'

Dave's dad lived in Pembrokeshire.

We looked again at the helicopters and police vans and began to question the barbecue smell. It was either delicious or reprehensible.

'What is it all about?'

'All I know is we have to leave.'

Michael and Kamara needed no more proof and they quickly began to put the twins into their double-width buggy. I liked the way the presence of these children meant we always had to assume the worst. Everything, everyone, was lethal. They made the world simple.

I cleared the paper plates, bottles, plastic wrappers, half-finished dips, even the real cutlery and made the decision – undiscussed but clear – to forego dividing it into reuse, recycle or landfill. I just shoved everything into a plastic bag and into the bin, all except for the coin and the drug vial, which I put in my own pocket, thinking that I would give them back to Dave later on, when things had calmed down, but also thinking that I wouldn't. Dave whipped up the blanket, balled it under his arm. Lee did not help. He stayed close to Marie, sharing more photos.

From the far side of the park, we saw a group of people – young people, judging by the speed with which they could run – some of whom had their faces covered, and they were sprinting our way. The park was almost empty and they were coming straight for us. Kamara and Michael stood in front of the twins' pram, he opening his shoulders, making himself big, and she communicating with her eyes that she was ready to kill. The young people ran towards us – then straight past us, along the path in the direction of the helicopters.

'Let's go to mine, it's closer,' Dave said, and we started off at pace, cutting straight over the bumpy grass. I was forced to regret all those years that I had mocked parents for their off-road-ready buggies, the ones with outsize, independently articulated wheels – *Where do these pricks think they are, Everest base camp?* – because I now saw that this vehicle handled well at speed over rough terrain. The twins were not even my children and I knew that I would die for them. How much stronger would these feelings be for my own child? It had been good while it lasted, this shallow, narcissistic life, but it was too late now. Soon I would be selfless.

Kamara pushed the buggy while Michael called taxi numbers on his phone, swearing under his breath at each engaged tone. The smell of burning got stronger as we crossed the park.

Marie and Lee were lagging. She was winding back and forth across the grass, trying to get away from him.

'I'm just *really* worried about William,' I heard him say. 'Let's go and check if he's okay. He lives in a flat above the pharmacy on Well Street.'

Marie ran ahead, past us, falling into shadow beneath trees at the exit of the park before turning on to Amhurst Road.

'I've got two baby girls here,' Michael said, yelling at the handset, holding it in front of his mouth like a police radio.

Outside the park, the street was overrun with non-threatening pedestrians. Everyone was looking up towards a red bus abandoned at an angle across the street and, beyond it, a vehicle on fire. Our favourite Turkish-Cypriot greengrocer was standing outside his shuttered-up shop, holding a length of banister in both hands like a baseball bat.

'What's going on?' I said.

'They burned the best car on the street,' he said.

There were people on their doorsteps and at their windows and standing on garden walls. The last time I'd seen the streets this busy it was the Queen's Golden Jubilee. The twins in their Guardsman sleepsuits kicked their legs. Michael screamed into his phone: 'You can't just leave us here!'

Just then, a row of six elegant police horses rounded the corner of Sandringham Road and came on to Amhurst. Even in the context of the wide street with its outsize Georgian terraces, the horses seemed huge, their neck muscles flexing, tails all combed straight and cut the same length. An atmosphere of taxes well spent.

'Thank God for the police,' Michael said, his phone at his side. 'Thank God for the police.'

A boy on a BMX said: 'What will horses do?'

I looked ahead and saw Marie flinch as Lee threw his phone against a wall. The screen shattered but the handset remained whole. He picked up the phone and chucked it again, as though the first throw had felt insufficiently destructive, and this time the casing cracked and came apart, which was *still* not enough so he kicked the wing mirror off a small red car. It came away in one. Trapezoids of glass fell to the pavement. Some people turned to look but said nothing. Lee's biceps were formidable. He kicked the space where the wing mirror had been, the coloured wires hanging loose. Then he started crying and sat down on the pavement, lit by the strobe of the car's hazards.

'I don't care what you do. You think I care but I don't,' he said.

Marie leaned against the red car.

It was interesting to note that their drama was probably only the fifth or sixth most exciting thing to look at.

Kamara and Michael were climbing into the front bench seat of a yellow van, each holding a twin tightly on their laps. In the driver's seat there was a stodgy, hairy-necked gentleman holding a lit cigarillo, clearly not a licensed taxi driver. The traffic light was red, but he ignored it and did a huge and ostentatious U-turn in the middle of the crosshatched zone, the normal rules of society giving way to chaos. As they came back past me at a careful speed, I saw the twins were inhaling sidestream smoke, which is three times more toxic and six times more tumorigenic than what the smoker himself inhales. You save them from one thing and they are killed by another.

Dave was on the phone. 'Allen,' he said. 'Are you okay?'

With the exception of Marie and Lee, everyone was engaged in locating or saving the people they loved. I called my wife. It was too noisy for us to hear each other clearly, so I just yelled at the handset that I was scared but I loved her and I would be waiting for her after work. The accompanying sound of sirens and helicopters gave my voice gravitas.

Garthene texted back: *Fucking scary. Be careful. xxx*

Three kisses in a row. I felt like a fruit machine.

When I turned back, Dave was running at pace down Amhurst with his phone to his cheek. I looked around for Marie and Lee but they'd gone, just the broken mirror blinking orange on the pavement.

Two hours until I needed to meet Garthene at the hospital.

Just off the high street, there was a small shop with its window smashed. I'd never noticed that it existed before, and couldn't tell from the sign what it sold. A man emerged with an electric heater. A man emerged with a tool set. The owner was sitting on the edge of the pavement with his head in his hands. While the burning cars had a visual purity, this was harder to like. I wanted to offer the shopkeeper my condolences, but his proximity to the action made him untouchable. There was an invisible line I couldn't bring myself to cross, so I stood with a group of my neighbours, watching from the opposite pavement; we all had our faces uncovered to signify neutral status. A woman in an apron crossed the road and put her arm around the shopkeeper; we all realized we could have done the same, but understood we'd missed our chance.

Beside me was a large man with badly executed neck tattoos who had a crate of beer at his feet. He offered me a can. It was the sort of lager I considered myself too good for.

'I'm fine, actually,' I said.

'No, you're not,' he said.

I chuckled because I was a little frightened, then took the can. I didn't want to seem like a tourist. 'Thank you,' I said.

'Don't thank me,' he said, and put another can in my coat pocket.

I felt uncomfortable and so drifted towards the vegan café, where there was a stand-off between a row of riot police and some people with bandanas and scarves wrapped around their heads, hoods up. A helicopter was circling, raising our expectations. We watched a tall boy lean over a low garden wall, pick a bottle out of a recycling box and throw it – brown glass, an ale, probably a microbrew – and it came down short and exploded on the road at the feet of the police. They lowered their visors and charged, boots crunching on the tarmac, shields glinting, batons aloft. My neighbours and I took a step back, able to both sympathize with the young people's frustrations while, at the same time, recognizing the police had a job to do.

I walked down Mare Street, sipping my cold beer. I watched a young man emerge from the phone shop, his hands full of handsets.

He threw them into the air and whooped as they clattered around him, batteries scudding on the pavement. Most businesses had their grates down. When I finished the first beer, I put the can in a recycling bin, enjoying my heightened lawfulness.

Down the road, people were photographing the looting of the Carhartt outlet. Carhartt is a good transitional brand for those like me who want to take a step towards adult clothing but not lose contact with the atmosphere of skateboarding. There was a disorderly queue of people squeezing in through the lifted shutter. You couldn't feel terrible about it. This was a discount outlet, so the clothes had, by definition, not been sold in the flagship on Carnaby Street and would probably be worth more via insurance. Plus, Carhartt were now reaching streetwise tastemakers who they would normally pay good money to attract, the kinds of people who can jimmy shutters with a socket wrench.

I finished the second beer while I was standing outside our estate agent's. I can't deny I was gratified to see one of the floor-to-ceiling windows had been smashed and there were four young men – two on the shoulders of two more – trying to pull a flat-screen off the wall. That the TV continued to function, showing twenty-four-hour rolling news, was a decent advertisement for Sanyo. On the screen, a banner read *BREAKING NEWS: London Burning as Rioters Torch Cars and Loot Shops* over live footage of the young men trying to take the TV off the wall. Then the men doing the yanking saw themselves on the screen – or, rather, saw their past selves, since the footage had a delay – and seeing how unconvincing they looked, began to pull harder. The flat screen's frame was fixed with four heavy-duty industrial bolts. They would need a special tool.

I stepped up to one of the unsmashed windows and saw, on a backlit display stand, a photo of the horrible maisonette, marked with a red triangle as SOLD (STC). I peered through at Dan's desk, which, as he had explained to me, he wasn't supposed to call *his* desk. They hot-desked and had a 'leave no trace' policy, so you weren't allowed to keep personal items – photos, toys, snacks – anything that would suggest residence. He said that, in reality, you could still *claim* a desk in all sorts of subtle ways, by affixing an expensive sun guard to the monitor or, in Dan's case, by leaving behind a box of disinfectant keyboard wipes. Not technically personal – although everyone knew they were Dan's – but also clever in the way they implied disgust at other people's fingers, grimy from shaking hands and handling keys. He had told me a story about two of his male colleagues who had fought a silent battle for the window desk with 'the corner-office feel', each getting in earlier than the other, earlier and earlier, until at some point – too early for anybody else to have been in the office to see – something happened, nobody knows what, and the victorious male was allowed everlasting dominion.

The TV news footage was useful because I could see that I was not in view of the camera. I ducked and slipped inside through the shattered glass, crouched out of sight behind the line of desks. The English champagne and two beers had given me access to a new version of myself. The workstations were tidy, staplers squared off beside Post-it notes. I knelt behind the one with the disinfectant wipes. In the top drawer there were pens and a postcard of low-lying mist in Milford Sound on New Zealand's South Island. In the larger, lower drawer, there were all the homes from A to Z. I found the horrible maisonette and pulled out the documents, laid them on the thin carpet. The names of the buyers were Mr Anders Timms and Ms Tavi Miniano and they were not even married. Anders was a designer, Tavi a computer programmer. They had a combined annual salary of £180,000. They already owned a property in Clerkenwell. My eyes settled on three words which changed everything. *Buy-to-let*. I let myself fill with anger, felt it line my insides. Small-scale landlords think nobody sees their quiet evil. It was almost funny how cruel it was to prevent us from owning our family home in order to rent it back to us. You could navigate from a morality this degraded. The couple's address was Flat 26, St John's Court, EC1 4TH. The *C* in the postcode stood for central. I photographed the documents with my phone. Crawling on all fours back towards the smashed window, I cut my palm on a small sliver of glass. A bead of red rose to the surface and I thought of how I might smear *DIE-TO-LET* in my own blood on the windscreen of the cash buyers' Qashqai.

It was still only seven thirty and I didn't want to arrive at the hospital early. I wanted to be out of breath from running when I met Garthene, give her a sense of how many threats I had overcome. I sat on the edge of the raised flower beds outside the town hall, feeling pleasantly unhinged. The sound of helicopters in the air matched the sensation in my head. I looked again at the *xxx* on my phone. They were kisses of fear or, rather, kisses *against* fear. The resilience of the human spirit. I thought of my parents, both born in 1943, just old enough that they both remember rationing, a fact they have been lording over me ever since. As the smell of burning thickened, I understood that they could never patronize me again.

But then, in the window of a car, I saw myself. It was disappointing. I did not look like a man in history. My eye was unbruised, my stitches dissolved. My brief holiday as a damaged person was over and now I was just a tech journalist with a forgettable face, dressed for a picnic. The cut on my hand was not even bleeding any more, just a little red dot you'd hardly notice. I took my keys from my pocket and worked the wound a little to get it going again.

Blood means nothing to Garthene unless in drinkable quantities. It seeped into the wrinkles on my palm.

Garthene stepped from the staff exit, held the railing and started down the stairs just as I crossed the hospital car park, my forehead sticky with sweat and smoke. We hugged on the steps then kissed hard, the first real-feeling kiss in some time.

'You okay?'

'Yes. You?'

'I'm good.'

'Your hand.'

'It's fine.'

'Let's see.'

I hoped we'd never again be polysyllabic. She held me at the wrist and I was fully expecting her to waft away the wound but instead she said 'Hold on' and went back inside. She came out with a disinfectant wipe and a large, professional gauze, cleaned the wound, then sealed it. Whatever we had needed to tell each other was irrelevant now. We had transcended language.

I had the key out before we got to our block. There was a knack to the main door and sometimes it took a couple of goes but not today. On the top landing, she pushed her bump against me. I could feel my pulse in my wounded right hand as I pressed it to her crotch. The smell of burning cars as we stepped inside the flat.

We stayed in the kitchen-lounge, ignoring Lee's belongings on every surface, ignoring our own bed. She kicked off her work shoes and pushed down her drawstring trousers and knickers all in one. A joyful lack of romantic formality. I did not remove my shirt, button by button, but took it off over my head like a T-shirt. I let my shorts fall. I had to pull the waistband of my boxer briefs up and over my penis in order to take them off. I had taken a long bath that morning, so my genitals were startlingly clean. You could eat your dinner off them. It was broadly canoe-shaped, my penis, widest in the middle, tapered ends. Garthene was naked from the waist down, which is even more naked than someone without clothes. She sat on the edge of the table, on the block print tablecloth, and I knelt. We could hear our phones ringing in our trouser pockets on the floor, and it helped to think of our parents fearing us dead. With my knees on the floorboards, I could feel the phones' vibrations pass pleasurably up through my legs and into my deep balls, my mother's worry alive inside me.

We didn't say a word to each other. She pulled her tunic over her head. I know it's uncool to find large breasts mesmerizing but sometimes you have to raise your hand and admit to being ruled by prehistoric instincts. I put my mouth between her legs, my vision completely filled by her bump. I could not see Garthene at all, had no idea of her facial expression, but I trusted that she was happy, relieved to finally work through my guilt. My view was pure womb, rising smooth and taut from her pubis, the strange dark line underneath the skin, her skin warm against my face, the red nipple of her outed belly button. I did not rush to the clitoris. There is more to life than the cold pursuit of measurable status markers.

She pulled me up to standing. I should say that neither Garthene nor I enjoyed being sexually experimental or degrading one another. People who pride themselves on having no boundaries always think those who choose not to tongue each other's arseholes and repurpose domestic objects are conforming to societal pressure. I think *they* are the orthodoxy – with their stamina rings, their mouths zipped shut – while it is couples like Garthene and I with bold, equipment-free intimacies who are brave, daring to look one another in the eye.

We got going and it was obscenely pleasurable. The best sex of our marriage during the worst civil disobedience in a generation. We hadn't made love in a while so I found it necessary to tug down my balls, a method from the Internet. She held me at the hips and yanked me in towards her, again and again, either fucking something into me or out of herself, hard to tell. The sound of our phones receiving voicemails and texts and calls, the pulse of our parents' terror. Mild pain in the palm of my hand. Family vehicles steadily aflame in the streets below.

And when I came I made a strange, choking noise. Garthene gripped my sides and ground herself against me and she came too. The only 100 per cent effective contraception is to have a baby up there already. We stayed like that until my penis shrank and slipped out, guiltily, in a hood. I leaned forward over her bump and we kissed and kissed and she was able to continue breathing. All was forgiven. We were in love again, her eyes a little damp, her sinuses clear.

'You smell that?' I said.

'The burning?'

'The burning.'

'I do.'

PART TWO

Telephones rang in our dreams.

When we woke the next morning, I had five missed calls from my father. I rang him from bed.

'You okay, Dad?'

'Pack your bags.'

'What's going on?'

'The police are expecting more trouble this evening.'

'We haven't even had breakfast yet.'

'It's not safe for you two in that place.'

That place was London.

He insisted on paying for us to get a black cab all the way to Lowestoft.

The moment we pulled up at their house, he emerged from the front door holding his wallet raised high in his hand. He licked his thumb, licked it more wetly than was necessary, before counting out the crisp twenties and passing them through the driver's window.

'I don't need change,' he said, shaking the man's hand, enjoying the atmosphere of wartime camaraderie.

My mother came out to the front step, her arms wide for a hug.

'You're home now,' she said. 'Nothing bad ever happens in Lowestoft! Now come inside and meet our guests.'

My parents' house was a five-bedroom converted windmill over-looking the stony beach. They moved here after I left for university. The ceilings were so low that I had to crouch in the doorways and duck between the beams while my father – who had begun to shrink – could glide around untouched. There was a sense they had deliberately bought a house with these dimensions so that I would never move back home.

Now that they had no responsibilities, they filled their lives with new interests. My father played the viol. Most weekends he prac-tised courtly waltzes with his early-music quintet. My mother painted. She painted skyscapes with her fingers, smearing the oils on thick, occasionally using a palette knife, never a brush. She was fearsomely productive. Rows of grim cloud banks stood drying in the garage.

A South Korean family had been staying with my parents for the last two days. The daughter, who was twelve, was a world-renowned solo violinist performing in my father's church as part of the Suffolk Festival. My parents enjoyed having performers to stay, took pleas-ure in their eccentricities – the poet who had sleep-climbed out through the skylight; the jolly, alcoholic Polish brass band who woke the nearest neighbours (half a mile away) with a fabulously woozy rendition of Liszt's Hungarian Rhapsody No. 2. My parents always told these anecdotes to new guests and said: *So you've got a lot to live up to!*

We all sat around the big table in the conservatory. My mother brought out an antipasti platter. She was wearing an embroidered kaftan and a wooden necklace. She also had a male-nipple-sized lump of livid pink scar tissue at the top of her chest from where the surgeon had clumsily removed a young tumour. I mention this only because she liked to make a feature of it, the scar, so had arranged her collar and necklace to frame the damage. *I like to make a feature of it* was one of her things to say.

'This is Seo-yun,' she said, signalling to the mother of the South Korean family, enunciating her name with elaborate clarity. 'She speaks wonderful English. And this is Ha-joon. And this is their daughter, Ji-yoo, though she also likes to use her Western name, June.'

'Nice to meet you all,' I said. 'I'm Ray.'

They each said my name in turn.

'And I'm Garthene.'

They didn't seem to find Garthene a weird or difficult name, which was refreshing.

'Even British people struggle to say Garthene!' my mother said, though this was not true, and it was just her who struggled, and not because she couldn't say it, rather that she just *didn't like* to say it. She preferred beautiful things, my mother – abstract sculpture, bowls of unusual stones – and had not yet found a way to say Garthene's name or even a shortened version of it – Garth, Gar, Gee – without using a cheerful or musical tone, as though trying to inject grace into something repellent. For a while, she even tried calling Garthene 'Jean' but gave up because it was clearly just a different name.

'Garthene is a nurse,' my mother said.

Whenever my mother introduces Garthene to someone, she immediately tells them she's a nurse, as though to make up for the fact that her name is Garthene.

'A nurse,' Seo-yun said, then she translated for her daughter and husband and they both looked at Garthene and made appreciative noises, then he asked a question.

'He would like to know your specialism,' Seo-yun said.

'I'm in ICU. The Intensive Care Unit.'

'That's the really bad one,' my mother said, leaning in.

'All the nasties,' my father said.

'Pneumonia,' my mother said.

'Haemorrhage,' my father said. He stuck his tongue out the side of his mouth, tilted his head and closed his eyes to signify a sudden, lethal brain injury. The Korean family laughed. Even though I often enjoyed telling people about Garthene's job, about her proximity to death, I didn't like to see my parents doing it.

'It's not that bad,' Garthene said.

'It really isn't,' I said. 'Fewer people die than you'd think.'

Seo-yun nodded but didn't translate for her family.

From the conservatory, there was a view straight out to sea, where it was starting to rain. To us Londoners, the dark clouds seemed exotic. Herring gulls were circling and, occasionally, tucking in their wings and plummeting from the sky.

'And what is your job, Ray?'

'Ray's an Internet journalist,' my mother said.

'He's a reviewer,' Garthene said. 'A critic.'

It was great to hear my wife stick up for me.

'Oh.' Seo-yun told Ha-joon and June. They widened their eyes and nodded.

'What is your specialism?' Seo-yun asked.

'Phones,' my mother said.

'The future,' Garthene said.

'The future!' my mother said, and she laughed, just at the thought of it.

The Korean family laughed too, but only out of politeness.

We talked some more. We learned that June was on a three-month world tour. This was her last stop in Europe before they headed to Toronto, Vancouver, then down the west coast. Her father did the accounts, bookings, visas. Her mother was in charge of June's home-schooling and could accompany her a little on the piano.

'But I am not a talented musician,' she said. 'I am useless. I don't know where she got it from.'

Then we all looked at June, who wore glasses, and had very white teeth, and slender pale fingers with which she was struggling to use the fork to spear a sun-dried tomato, this girl whose dexterity had won her a scholarship to the Yehudi Menuhin School. She looked up to find us all staring at her, amazed and scared of her talent, her youth, and she turned to her mother for an explanation, which she gave her, in two short sentences, after which the daughter smiled, blushed and looked down at her plate.

We went up to our room. It was a room we'd never slept in before. The third spare room. The idea that my parents had rooms I'd hardly seen, let alone spent the night in, was disturbing. We watched the sea from the window. The waves were always noisy here, raking up the stones and throwing them down, sounding like a chip tray sinking into hot oil.

We heard the young violinist practising. It came up through the floor. She was playing something slow and sweeping, but with occasional ripples of eloquent quick notes. Her music displayed an emotional intelligence, an honesty of expression, that put into shameful context our small talk around the dining table.

Garthene and I sat on the bed to listen.

'Classical music's good for the baby,' I said.

I put my hand on her bump. She put her hand on top of mine.

'What if our child is incredibly talented?' she said.

'It seems unlikely.'

'But what if? Such a responsibility.'

'I know,' I said. 'Up at the swimming pool, six in the morning.'

'Standing beside the tennis court, hands raw from clapping, six days a week. For decades.'

'All the equipment. A Stradivarius.'

June's violin was not even a Stradivarius and still it was insured for one and a half million dollars. My father had whispered the figure to us when he showed us to our room. 'Her violin is worth more than this house,' he'd said, 'and she carries it around in a soft case — terrifying!' People who have loads of money love to talk about people who have even more, in order to try on the costume of poverty.

'At least our child will dedicate their greatest work to us, later on,' Garthene said.

'When they accept an award?'

'Yeah. Or win a grand slam.'

'Most of all I want to thank my parents.' I leaned down and spoke to the bump. 'Without them I would never be where I am now.'

'They gave up so much for me to thrive.'

'They abandoned their lives. They lost everything.' I was still talking to our unborn child.

'Everything?'

'Everything.'

We looked at each other.

Through the floorboards there came the sound of a gorgeous extended tremolo, the note high and true.

That evening, we watched the news. A presenter stood at the end of our street. We had forgotten completely about our burning city.

'There's our flat,' Garthene said.

Seo-yun looked at Garthene but seemed not to have understood. Or perhaps had understood, but didn't believe it. The screen showed images of cars on fire. It showed footage of those boys trying to steal the flat-screen from the estate agent's. I was presumably just out of frame.

'This isn't a very good advert for our country,' my father said, and he changed the channel.

There were more burning vehicles on both ITV and Channel 4. There was a topical news quiz on BBC Two. There was a Hollywood film starring Cate Blanchett on Channel 5. He turned off the TV.

The violin was on the table between us, in its soft case.

My dad stared at it.

'It's a wonderful instrument,' he said.

'Thank you,' Seo-yun said.

'Seo-yun was telling us about the wolf note,' my mother said.

Seo-yun smiled.

'A wolf note is one note on a violin which makes a kind of howling sound,' my mother said.

'*Ow-wow-wow-wow-wow*,' my dad said, and everyone laughed.

'Which note is it again?'

Seo-yun asked June, who replied.

'It's a G sharp,' Seo-yun said.

My father turned to us. 'Some musicians try to avoid violins that have wolf notes, but June says she prefers it this way. She says that a strong wolf gives the rest of the instrument a clarity of tone.' He then put on a Shakespearean voice. 'One note suffers so the rest can stay pure.'

'Though sometimes she puts a special device on the violin to *neutralize the wolf*!' my mother said.

'Just the language of it,' my father said.

'Wonderful,' my mother said.

'What's the note called in Korean?' my father said.

'We just call it the broken note.'

'Oh, okay,' my father said. 'Still.'

Later, Garthene and I were in bed in the third spare room. The bed was actually two single mattresses covered with a king sheet. It wasn't possible to cuddle without one person having the feeling that they were falling down into a sinkhole.

'We're going to be great parents,' I said.

'I hope so.'

'I kind of hate my job anyway,' I said, 'so I'd be happy to have our child completely fill my otherwise empty life.'

'That's good to know.'

'I'm willing to throw my career on the bonfire of our child's extraordinary talent.'

We each put a hand on her belly. The baby shifted its exceptional hips.

'Percussionist,' she said.

'Judo master.'

We lay there.

'Would you really give up everything?' she said.

I wanted to give her the right answer.

'Of course,' I said.

She looked up at the ceiling. I watched her face for clues.

'Was that the right answer?' I said.

'I actually don't know,' she said.

The next day, before we returned home, we went to June's concert. My father stood at the front of the church and introduced her.

'With everything that is going on in our country, it is a

wonderful privilege to turn our attention to gentler things. We have with us today a young woman who, at twelve years old, is already one of the world's great players. She is not only technically immaculate, but offers emotional insight rarely heard in players three times her age. Please welcome to the stage Pak Ji-yoo.'

We had to sit in the front row. The pews were uncomfortable, particularly for Garthene. Every time she shifted her body the wood made a sad mewing noise.

June began with a very fast, very impressive piece by Paganini. Her posture was incredible. Her hand seemed like a separate animal, like a time-lapse video of a spider preparing its web. Her parents sat next to us and their gaze never once dropped from their daughter's kind face. Next she played a slow, mournful one. She swayed a little, completely lost to the music. This was a girl who, as far as I knew, had no actual life experience. She'd presumably never fallen in love or had sex or had her heart broken or seen someone die or been punched in the face. And yet she seemed to truly comprehend melancholy. She comprehended it in more depth than I did. And my city was burning. That wasn't even a metaphor. My life was in actual flames. And still I couldn't find the music moving.

The wooden pew beneath me groaned and I looked across to see Garthene's eyes were wet. It was bad of me to think that her extra emotional sensitivity was due only to surging hormones. But I did think that. Under normal circumstances, I thought, she and I would be unified in our emotional deadness.

At the end of the concert, June got a standing ovation. It's easy to get a standing ovation when the seats are so uncomfortable. Nevertheless, she deserved it. She was only twelve years old. She gave three deep bows, then my father brought her flowers.

'Wasn't she just *magnificent*?' he said.

PART THREE

We emerged from our front door to join the clean-up effort, me holding an old-fashioned broom across my chest, Garthene with a dustpan and brush, both of us carrying a dark secret, that we felt refreshed from our mini-break at the seaside.

There were already six people out in front of the Safeway, four sweeping up small granules of glass and two dealing with big shards, kneeling on the sunny pavement in gardening gloves. A woman shattered the outsize shapes with a tiny hammer; a man wrapped them in newspaper. It looked like a satisfying job. The inside of the shop was empty, cordoned off with police tape. We hovered for a moment, hoping to feel useful, then went around the corner to the hardware store.

The owner, the man who I'd failed to hug, was being inter-viewed on the forecourt, saying: 'I believe most people are kind,' and the small shop was full of volunteers in old T-shirts drilling shelves and bleaching the floor, one tall, gaunt man replacing strip lights, a camerawoman tracking through the cramped aisles.

Over at the abandoned red bus, which was still beached in the middle of the road, we saw a large group of people with brooms, some raising theirs into the sky and cheering. For a moment it seemed spontaneous and heart-warming, but then we heard the photographer asking that the shortest people come forward.

We walked on a bit further and saw the car with the wing mirror that Lee had kicked off. Sadly, a couple were already kneeling there on the pavement.

'We should have come back earlier,' I said.

'Relax,' Garthene said. 'We'll find something.'

When we got closer we recognized the couple. It was Marie and Lee, both wearing rubber gloves and walking boots, his hair dark and greasy, hers tied tight to the scalp. We watched them for a while, their careful, quiet attention, Lee holding open the bag while Marie dropped each piece in, the glass chattering. There was a touching intimacy to their actions. Once they'd finished clearing up the glass, they held each other's eyes for a moment, then began to kiss. It was endearing at first and then quickly not endearing. They gripped the backs of each other's heads in a way that, if their heads had not been there, would have been an arm wrestle. Their tongues thrashed around between them. Through the rips in his jeans, Lee was bare-kneed on the rough tarmac, which must have been uncomfortable, yet he maintained absolute focus. The sexual chemistry Garthene and I had attained seemed suddenly feeble. Probably the whole city had been hard-fucking in lesser-used rooms.

'Well, this *is* romantic,' Garthene said.

They detached, looked at us and started laughing. As we hugged them, their rubber gloves squeaked disturbingly behind our backs.

'Shouldn't you be killing each other?' I said.

'We almost did,' Marie said.

'Don't worry,' Lee said and he kissed Marie's cheek. 'There's still time.'

'We haven't forgiven each other,' she said. 'He's a total maniac.'

'I am,' Lee said. 'And yet she's the one who found a new boy-friend in under seven days.'

'I'm thirty-seven,' she said. 'No time to waste.'

They laughed. We enjoyed their self-awareness.

'Well, it's good to see you two together,' Garthene said.

'It is,' I said. 'Have you found anything that we could clean up?'

Lee came close to my ear. 'I'm not proud of what I did,' he said, with a smile in his voice, 'but there might still be some damage to a grey Honda parked on the road by the primary school.'

Both wing-mirror casings were hanging loose, the shattered glass glittering. That cheered us up and we worked in silence, triple-bagging it. I saw glimpses of my wife reflected in the shapes of mirror on the road, a patch of her forehead, a shoulder, the mystery of a nostril, and I loved it all.

On the way home, we bumped into our downstairs neighbour, Lindsey. Though we'd been in our flat for two years, Garthene and I had hardly spoken to her, just an occasional hi as we slid past on the stairs. I only knew her name from signing for her packages. Garthene and I liked to spy on her recycling, the lonely rice-pudding pots, the breakfasts in cans. We made mean jokes about her physique, how she went beyond pear-shaped into the more obscure silhouettes of the rare-breed squashes at the farmers' market. But that was old us. Now we were kind and open-minded nearly-parents, invested in society.

'How *are* you, Lindsey?' I said. 'It's good to see you.'

'I'm surviving. How are you two?'

'We're also surviving.'

'Are you going to the tea party?'

'What tea party?'

'I'll show you.'

This was it. *This* was community.

There were trestle tables along one side of the street with free cake, flans and quiche. There was calypso playing from speakers wedged in the open windows of the flat above the second-hand baby-clothes shop. Marie and Lee were in a group of people dancing and I could see no light between them. The back of Lee's T-shirt said *Detroit Techno Militia*. Children laughed as they practised hula hoop on the pavement. Two little girls were chalking *We Spread Love* in the space where a burning car had been; the blackened road had that almost-damp look, like when you lift up a stone in the garden. If you have a garden.

I thought for a moment about the horrible maisonette but found it hard now to resent the cash buyers. They were not property developers. They were not the ones turning every church, school and hospital into luxury flats. They simply wanted to carve out a little security for themselves in a dangerous world, and didn't I want the same? It occurred to me then that we should have asked my parents for money. When we were in Lowestoft, with the BBC presenter standing outside our London flat, the priceless violin on the coffee table, that would have been the moment to ask for monetary aid.

'At some point you just have to say,' I said quietly to Garthene, 'okay, I give in, I accept that I come from a background of financial liquidity. I am willing to live with that privilege.'

Garthene looked at me. 'You just have to say that, do you, at some point?'

'I think so,' I said.

Coming slowly up the street was one of those billboard trucks which normally advertise strip clubs but, on this occasion, there was a row of five grainy colour images of people and the words *Shop a Looter* beside a phone number for the local police. I looked at the photos of the looters. Four men, one woman. One of the men was wearing skate shorts – possibly Carhartt – which seemed amusing.

I ate a yum-yum from the trestle table and took two more for Garthene and Lindsey. Yum-yums are wonderfully trashy. All the food and drink at the tea party had been supplied by Marks & Spencer. There were bowls of Percy Pigs. The big joke with Percy Pigs is that they are made with pig gelatine. It's the honesty that people like.

The billboard truck came to the end of the road and parked.

Shop a Looter. It was a good line, considering they can't have had long to design it. I gave Garthene and Lindsey their yum-yums, then walked over to take a closer look at the billboard. It was a bit embarrassing but the looter with the shorts was wearing a shirt that I own, the off-white one with tiny blue dots. Of all the suspects, he was the easiest to hate. He had a can of lager in one hand, another in his pocket. He looked picnic-ready, smiling. I wasn't too proud to recognize a bit of myself in him and then slowly recognize all of myself in him because I was him and he was me, my own personal self.

There had clearly been some misunderstanding, I decided. A misunderstanding so profound it was funny. *Ha*, I thought, without actually laughing. To see my image travel through the borough on a signboard normally reserved for gentlemen's clubs. My own self blown up twice my actual size and broadened – a trick with the aspect ratio – so that I looked slightly buff. I sensed the heft of an anecdote. I was a wanted man. They wanted me. It was just a shame that in the photo I looked so pleased about it. There must have been other images they could have used.

The truck moved slowly on, disappearing behind the betting shop.

I went back to stand beside Lindsey and Garthene, their lips now sugared, both bouncing gently to sunshine reggae.

When we got home, I ran Garthene a bath, pouring in a large scoop of Norwegian minerals. Those crystals were so expensive that I knew she would feel duty-bound to soak for hours, giving me enough time to clarify everything with the police. Once she was in the water, I got my keys, wallet and passport – did the police like to see a passport? I had no idea! – and quickly went out to the station at the bottom of Clapton Square. *The cop shop*, I thought to myself, enjoying language previously unavailable to me. I jogged there, trying to carry my sense of humour, my giggling disbelief, while it still glowed in my throat. But the station was shut, permanently, metal anti-squat cages covering the windows. I noticed a sign from a property developer with a phone number to call for off-plan sales.

After that I caught the 488 down to the bigger station in Bow. It was difficult to maintain light-hearted incredulity for the entire bus journey and, for a few moments, as we waited in traffic on the Whitechapel Road, I put my forehead against the cool metal handrail and the idling engine's vibrations transmitted waves of terror through my skull. I got out my phone and looked through the photos I had taken of the estate agent's documents, then deleted them. I found Dave's liquid drugs in the pocket of my jeans. I left the vial on the seat for some lucky traveller. I looked at my wounded hand. A little dot of red had worked its way through the gauze. I peeled it off and, underneath, my hand was completely fine.

I got off the bus and made myself cheerful again as I approached the station, an elaborate Victorian red-brick building with wide steps bordered by gas lamps that had *POLICE* written in the blue-tinted glass. I let the thought of Garthene in the tub carry me up the stone stairs, a skip in my step, the casual grace of a married man coming to clear up a small misunderstanding.

Through the booth's plastic glass a woman of about my age was looking down at a form, her hair tightly centre-parted, a clear avenue of scalp.

'Hello,' I said.

She didn't look up. 'How can I help?' she said.

'I've come to, well, *I've come to hand myself in*,' I said, modulating my voice to signify the ridiculousness.

When she looked up, I raised my hands in surrender.

'What have you done?' she said.

'Nothing, actually. I'm a journalist. And I was reporting on the disturbances – the riots.'

She raised her eyebrows, three smooth equidistant ridges forming on her forehead, like waves taking shape out at sea.

'But there's obviously been some kind of mistake because I just saw my picture on a poster.' I pointed out to the street behind me and chuckled. 'It said *Shop a Looter*, which is a great tagline, by the way. So I thought I'd better come and' – I paused for effect – 'get shopped.'

She waited to make sure I had finished speaking, then she smiled. She had a gap between her front teeth, a keyhole view into the darkness of her throat.

'That's very good of you,' she said.

She rustled around in a desk drawer and brought out the poster with the five images.

'I'm the one drinking,' I said. 'I don't even like lager.'

She squinted from the picture to me and back again. 'I'm going to have to put you under arrest, for now anyway. I hope you understand.'

'That's totally reasonable,' I said. 'It would be wrong to just take my word for it. But I hope we can get this dealt with fairly quickly.'

She nodded. 'You're under arrest. What you say can be used as evidence.'

'I didn't realize you actually had to do that bit.'

'Oh, we do.'

'Will you put me in handcuffs as well?' I said. 'Will you *cuff* me?'

'Not unless you think it's necessary.'

'Well, it might be,' I said. 'I might be a career criminal. A lunatic.'

She leaned forward a little. 'You might be,' she said.

It was wonderful to take part in this interaction. I made my eyes wide and vibrated my head left and right, as I imagine murderers do.

'Okay,' she said. 'Come through to the back room.'

There's a mugshot of Bill Gates from 1977, taken by Albuquerque police, where he is wearing yellow-tinted shades and his hair is gorgeously, goldenly coiffed, like an astronaut's helmet glowing in the warmth of the sun. He looks happy, some of his white teeth showing, not a full-blown grin, but enough that you know he is glad the arrest has given shape to his life. His tan is mellow, the police ID board hung around his neck like a medal. He was arrested for a traffic violation. It was comforting to wonder whether he would ever have gone on to do so much good without the memory of this transgression throbbing warmly inside him. Would the Bill & Melinda Gates Foundation's many philanthropic projects – Senegalese family-planning clinics and women-only toilets in Indian slums – have ever existed if that state trooper had failed to pull him over on a day just before Christmas, on the interstate between Texas and New Mexico?

My officer's name was Dana and we were hitting it off. Her parents were Nigerian. Nigerians are one of the most high-performing immigrant groups, not that I wouldn't have liked her if she'd had roots elsewhere. We were in a small office, a raised wooden counter dividing the room in two, me on one side, she on the other.

'I've got a part-Nigerian friend,' I said. 'Kamara.'

'Is that so?'

'Yes. I love her. She's great. She's Igbo.'

'Okay. Well, tell her I said hi.'

There might have been a touch of sarcasm, but I let it slide. She held up the webcam.

'Get my good side,' I said.

She made a show of examining my face. 'They're all bad.'

'Hey, that's prejudice. I could have your badge for that.'

'We don't have badges.'

This was brilliant. It was that same joyous feeling I get while speaking to a doctor. I always have to go shopping after a medical appointment just to ride out the adrenaline.

'You know that other thing people always say in films after they've been arrested?'

'I want my lawyer?' she said.

'No. The other *I want my*. I want my . . . ?'

'Mummy?'

'Phone call.'

'Oh, yeah. They say that. You don't get a phone call though.'

'What about a text message?' I said. '*I want my SMS.*'

She smiled and shook her head. Her gappy teeth were fashionable.

'Oh, man,' I said. 'You're tough. How long do you think all this'll take, anyway?'

'Why? Have you got a train to catch?'

'Absolutely,' I said, 'if by *a train* you mean a pregnant wife and by *catch* you mean provide emotional support for.'

'Ho,' she said.

'Will I be home for dinner is what I'm asking?'

'No chance.'

'Come on.'

'We'll need you overnight and then we decide if we're going to charge you.'

'Dana, that's crazy.'

She looked at me. I could see something in that sentence had wound her up, so I tried again.

'*Officer*, that's crazy,' I said.

'Look. We're taking your involvement seriously.'

'I wouldn't call it involvement.'

'What would you call it?'

'Observation. Tourism. Heavy looking. The thing is, my pregnant wife is in the bath right now and soon she'll get out and her lumbar region won't moisturize itself.'

'Is that a police problem?'

'You haven't met my wife!'

It was an end-of-the-pier-type joke and Dana didn't go for it. There was a shift in tone. I held up my hands again. 'Will you at least let me text her? She's a nurse, you know. Front-line services, just like you.'

Dana closed her eyes. She sighed, disappeared into the back room, brought my phone through and handed it to me. She did not avert her eyes as I typed in my unlock code. I'd been using the same number since I was fifteen and very earnest, when I'd chosen a security pin for my first bank account. Two, zero, four, six. It made the sign of the cross on the keypad, as a way to comment on society's reverence for capital. My online banking password was *abandon_hope_all_ ye_who*, so then you had to press Enter.

'And just before I write this I'm going to be totally honest with you, Dana, and admit that I'll be telling my wife a teensy little white lie.'

Her expression did not change.

'I don't want her to get stressed. That's important when you're pregnant.'

Dana's eyes stayed steady. I started typing. She stood beside me so she could see the message as I wrote it. It was difficult under pressure.

Gutted! Jake needs me to cover the launch of a new Nokia in Hel-sinki. :-(I'm on my way to Stansted! I didn't want to interrupt your bath! Love you. Back tomorrow! x x x

I handed Dana the phone.

'Is she going to believe that?' she said.

'I think so,' I said. 'Because of how I have no track record for lying.'

They wrote out my statement in a small, well-lit office room, Dana and a male officer named Liam, who had a childlike face. His eye-lashes were remarkable, like tiny brooms.

He said: 'We appreciate your helping us.'

She said: 'Really we do.'

It was the good cop, good cop routine.

The desk in one corner was reassuringly messy, sheets of carbon paper loosely piled, a lidless highlighter pen drying out beneath a swing arm lamp.

I talked them through the full day in question, trying to give a

sense of journalistic thoroughness: picnic, helicopters, kids sprinting, a bus ditched in the middle of the road, a vehicle in flames, a
hardware store pillaged, riot police doing a good job in difficult
circumstances, a gift of beer, handset confetti, how violent disorder
fits well with Carhartt's brand of urban vigilantism, how I had
stepped through shattered glass into the estate agent's in order to
get a clearer angle for a photograph of the crime in progress. That
was my one lie. I allowed myself that. As I said it, I noted a small
change in their expressions, so I decided to give the lie some colour. I talked about how much a good news photo is worth when a
story goes worldwide, like this one. I said my heavily pregnant
wife the nurse and I needed the money. I went on to mention the
photo of the Tank Man of Tiananmen Square, how the guy who
shot that image now lives off the royalties.

'One man protests repression in Beijing,' I said, lifting my voice
a little, 'and another buys a beach house in San Diego. It's crazy.'

Liam had stopped taking notes. I'd managed to turn good cop,
good cop into sad cop, tired cop. There was a sense they were both
thinking of other careers. It was easy to imagine Dana working in
events, Liam a driving instructor. Dana took me downstairs and
put me in a holding cell. I spoke to her through the slat in the door.

'You don't think I'll get charged, do you?'

'Not up to me.'

'Not up to you? *Why not?*' I raised my voice. 'You're the best
damn cop in this whole precinct.'

'You're a character,' she said.

'But if it were up to you, you wouldn't charge me, right?'

'Probably not,' she said. 'You'd just clog up the system.'

'I would,' I said. 'Bung it right up.'

She blinked.

'Sorry. I just feel we have a great rapport,' I said.

'Sleep well.' The slat slid closed.

'Guilty people sleep well,' I said, 'so I'll sleep really badly.'

Murderers sleep deeply after their arrest because it's a relief to get caught. The innocent lie awake with the fear of wrongful conviction. And what about those of us in a third, unadvertised category who agree they have done wrong in the eyes of the law but believe it was something small and understandable and sleep for a dreamless six hours with full faith in the justice system?

I woke when Dana knocked, glimpsing the gap in her teeth through the gap in the metal door. 'Rise and shine. You've been charged with aggravated trespass and handling stolen goods.'

'You're kidding,' I said.

'Sorry,' she said. 'But at least it'll be dealt with quickly. Riot-related offences are being fast-tracked.'

She wasn't lying. The magistrates' court was opposite the police station. It was a squat modern building made of brick the colour of bread. I followed Dana as she strode across the road, her handcuffs glinting in the sunshine. We descended to a windowless basement room with plastic seats that resembled a bingo hall. I sat with a dozen or so others awaiting justice, all much younger than me, mostly boys, some with legal aid, some with mental-health workers, one Chinese-looking kid with a puffy jacket who wanted us all to know he was representing himself. 'I represent myself,' he said. Above our heads hung the judicial coat of arms – a lion and a unicorn; one real, one mythical.

My defence lawyer was a woman in her forties, Antonia, whose scalloped nostrils allowed tasteful glimpses of purplish capillaries, a nose I instantly trusted. I was to be charged with accepting the stolen beers and entering the estate agent's. Antonia said that, under normal circumstances, I would plead not guilty and go to

Snaresbrook for trial, but that these circumstances were not normal and the judges were *on tilt*.

I had such fond memories of jury service, of how I and the other jurors had ganged up on the one woman who thought the guy was guilty, of how we had made her say it out loud – 'He just looks like he did it' – before working on her, needling her, using all kinds of musical and condescending tones of voice, a real team effort, until she cried. We set the guy free. He fell to his knees in the courtroom thanking God, which was us.

'So you think I should say guilty?'

'That would be my advice. They've got you on camera. I doubt they'll give you a custodial.'

'Custodial means jail?'

'Right.'

'What other options do I have?'

'Plead innocence, go to trial, roll the dice.'

'And how long would the trial take?'

'We won't get a court date for a month or two.'

'I'm having a baby in eight weeks' time.'

'Then go guilty,' she said. 'I'll work the baby into my statement.'

I sat behind inch-thick glass at the side of the courtroom. Dana was sitting beside me, openly yawning. The yawn went viral: I watched the young clerk's jawline pulse, then it spread to the usher, whose teeth popped right out, so he covered his mouth with both hands. This was good news. Chains of yawns are evidence of empathy.

We waited while some documents were photocopied. By the time the clerk called my name, Dana's eyes were shut, her breathing slow. It had been a tough few days, but I was still amazed she could sleep. It indicated that she valued my destiny less than I had imagined. All around me there was the oppressive boredom of the administrative staff, the mundanity of watching endless lives ruined.

One of the magistrates was an old, pink-headed white guy with neck flesh like drawn-back curtains and the other was a middle-aged black woman in a sober shirt-dress. They both looked supremely reasonable, listening with their heads tilted as the prosecutor summarized the police report. 'At 5.55 p.m., Mr Ray Morris was seen taking receipt of and proceeding to drink two cans of Carling lager, handed to him by a Mr Colin Barry, who this court saw yesterday. The beer had been looted from the nearby off-licence . . .'

The problem with my I-am-listening face is that it takes a lot of concentration to maintain. It's not possible to listen *and* look like I am.

'. . .Though he was not seen to have stolen any specific items from the estate agent's, it was clear that he was facilitating and supporting the widespread destruction of private and public property. And we see by his expression in this photo that Mr Morris *enjoyed* taking part in the worst unrest in our country for two decades.'

Unrest was a strange word. It made it all sound like nothing a nap couldn't fix.

When it was her turn, my lawyer really milked the baby thing – 'looking forward to being a first-time father at thirty-three' – and the community angle – 'just yesterday morning, Mr Morris and his wife were out on the streets with a dustpan and brush' – and she occasionally glanced across, signalling towards me with her open hand, during which moments I angled my gaze meekly downwards.

The magistrates' chairs squealed as they slid back from their desks to confer. Dana woke up and looked startled to find herself here, approaching middle age in an underfunded police force at the beginning of the third millennium.

The magistrates rolled back to their desks.

'Will the defendant please rise?'

I floated up towards the ceiling.

A small fine!

An electronic tag on my ankle the size of a diving watch!

A hundred hours of community service, which was something I'd been meaning to do for years anyway!

I wafted down the halls of Thames Magistrates' Court, admiring the pocked surface of the ceiling insulation panels, the way light from the high windows set aflame the civic handrails.

For the next eight months, I was not allowed to leave my flat during the hours of darkness!

No parties! No gallery openings! No theatre!

Only matinees!

It felt like freedom, this sentence. It felt more like freedom than real freedom had ever felt.

'Thank you so much.' I hugged Dana.

'Don't thank me.'

I went straight to the administrative office to pay my fine in full. Two hundred and fifty pounds plus a hundred in court fees.

'Can I use a credit card?' I said.

'You can,' she said.

'This one gets double air miles.' I was trying to mock my own entitlement but it didn't fly. She handed me the card reader. No gratuity option or I would have tipped the judicial system.

Walking down Bow Road, I was happy that the tag ruined the silhouette of my narrow jeans. I would have to buy different trousers now, wider trousers, and that felt absolutely right. I went to the British Heart Foundation and flicked through a rack of men's jeans, all the heartbreakingly normal body shapes, sad and varied. I pulled out a pair of eye-blue bootcut Lees, completely undistressed. I put them on in the changing room. Normal trousers are brilliantly comfortable – that's what they don't tell you.

'I'd like to buy the ones I'm wearing and donate these,' I said.

She held my old jeans up, let the legs unfurl.

'There's nothing wrong with them,' I said. 'In fact, they were quite expensive. It's just that they don't fit me any more, ideologically.'

I walked back into the street in normal trousers, coming to terms with the fact that I was still someone who could not resist adding the word *ideologically*.

I went to call Garthene and saw I had three messages, all from last night. The first read: *Product launch? You poor thing. Helsinki? Hellish. x* The second read: *Why don't you have a foreign dial tone?* The third message: *The police are here. They're looking for you.* There were no more messages, just missed calls, six from Garthene and one from a withheld number. Then my phone died in my hand.

As I climbed the stairs to our flat I began to feel the weight of the tag, how it altered my gait. By the time I got to the top, my legs felt unwieldy, out of sync with each other.

'Sweetheart?' I said as I opened the door, and then again, 'Sweetheart?' as I went into the kitchen-lounge, and so on, through the bathroom and bedroom, 'Sweetheart?' There were so few rooms to explore. I plugged in my phone and called Garthene but she didn't answer. Then I called her again and she'd switched her phone off. I sent six small messages: *I'm sorry. / I can explain. / I spoke to the police. / Everything's fine. / I'm at home. / I love you. xxx*

At ten thirty I heard a car outside and went to the window. There was a blue Vauxhall Astra idling, exhaust fumes lit red in the brake lights. Garthene was holding the passenger side door open and speaking into the car.

I went to stand at the top of the concrete stairwell. I'd never known her ascend so slowly. Her hand gripped the metal banister, properly put weight on it, in a way that made me realize I only ever held the banister as an affectation. Carrying our child put the discomfort of my tag into context. She paused on each landing. At one point she looked up and the despondency in her expression sent me back inside.

I put the baking dish out on a cork mat. I'd made lasagne, Garthene's favourite meal, also her death-row meal. I'd set a fat white candle burning in a clamp jar, but now it seemed inappropriately romantic, that I'd misjudged the mood. I licked my thumb and forefinger and snuffed it out, a thread of smoke unravelling. That left a burning smell, so I opened both windows to get a through-breeze. On hot nights like this the flies come up off the communal bins and three of them immediately entered, but none of this – the smell, the wind, the flies – registered with Garthene as she came in without comment, lowered herself into a chair at the table and waited for me to explain myself.

'I'm not going to prison,' I said.

'But,' she said.

'But.' I lifted my trouser leg. 'I can't leave the flat after darkness for the next eight months.'

She turned to the open window. She was wearing one of my baggy jumpers, though I sensed that she had chosen it purely from pragmatism.

'And I'm sorry I said I was in Helsinki. I didn't want to stress you. The police thought that I was involved in the unrest.'

'They told me. They came looking for you.'

'I'd already handed myself in.'

'There were three of them in here. They stood around me as I phoned you.'

'I'm sorry.'

'Why were you in the estate agent's?'

'I just wanted some information. About the cash buyers.'

'Ray.'

'They're *buying to let*. They've already got a place in Clerkenwell.'

'What were you planning to do?'

'Nothing bad. Just write them a passive-aggressive letter, like a normal human being.'

She didn't find me funny. She kicked off her shoes. My ankle was tagged and hers was lost to swelling.

'Where have you been?' I said.

'The hospital,' she said.

'I thought you weren't working –'

'I wasn't.'

She looked at me. I was being asked to jump to a conclusion. I didn't want to jump.

'Is anything wrong?' I said.

'I had pain,' she said.

'What kind?'

'Abdominal.'

I looked at her bump. Her hands were not touching it.

'Oh Christ,' I said.

'The doctor said I was having Braxton Hicks.'

She scanned my face for recognition. Braxton Hicks were, as far as I could remember, practice contractions and nothing to worry about, but the risk of guessing wrong, of underselling her condition, kept me quiet.

'They're practice contractions,' she said.

'I was going to say that.'

'They're normal.'

'That's what I thought. So the baby's –'

'Fine,' she said.

I nodded. 'And who took you to the hospital?'

'A colleague.'

I was not allowed to use this moment for accusations. 'That was nice of him or maybe her,' I said.

More flies had come in and were making weirdly orderly laps of the room. They were restless, high on bin juice. The best way to get them was with the device we kept beneath the sink, a battery-powered tennis racket with electrified strings that we bought on the Internet. While Garthene ate lasagne – her fork clattering against the plate, almost no visible signs of chewing – I swung the racket. It killed the smaller flies in a fizz of blue sparks but only burned the wings off the bigger ones. They dropped down and walked around the room on foot. It somehow didn't seem right to stomp on them, so I trapped each one under a glass, slid a postcard underneath, then took them to the window and let them, wingless, fall four storeys, live out their short lives on the street.

Garthene went straight to bed and I got in beside her. It seemed to me that the structure of pillows she used to support her stomach's weight and allow her knees and ankles to rest at a comfortable elevation now also functioned as a partition. When I woke in the middle of the night, I found her sitting upright, staring, working through a packet of water biscuits, the motion of her jaw shifting the mattress.

The next morning, the door buzzer rang. A large, bald man from Serco came upstairs carrying a tool bag and a black, buttonless box the size of a modem. Garthene and I followed him as he measured the flat's dimensions with a laser pen. Our minuscule flat. It was cruel to be under house arrest when I could not afford an actual house, jailed inside the very reason for my jailing.

'If you leave the flat after dark, Mr Morris, then this box will notify us.'

'Okay,' I said.

'And if you tamper with anything it will tell us about that too.'

'I won't do that.'

'Though if you go outside and come back within five minutes, you're okay. There's a grace period. If you need to take the bins out or sign for a package or –'

'Commit a really quick crime,' I said.

Tough crowd.

My wife and the man from Serco shared a look.

My community service began on Monday. I knelt beside the towpath with my fellow convicts, sweating, wearing a high-visibility waistcoat over a council-branded T-shirt. We clipped the brambles to stubs, tore out handfuls of nettles, scratched by the former, stung by the latter, but all pain was good. In my head, I repeated the names of my fellow convicts as an improving mantra: Aaron, Connor, Dave, Dave, Rich, Vishak, Vasile. We uncovered a rotting wooden ladder, a tricycle, sheets of metal, cans of a prehistoric fizzy drink called Enjoy. We talked as we worked. Vasile was an ex-professional cyclist from Romania. His torso was miraculously round, so spherical that it came close to aesthetic perfection, only spoiled by his head and limbs. He brought out a hip flask of vodka and we passed it around until it was empty.

At lunch, we sat side by side on benches by the river amid the sound of swans barking and the soft clack of our teeth. We hung our high-visibility waistcoats from the branches of a tree to breathe, the words *Community Payback* turning in the breeze.

During the afternoon, we cleared more of the towpath, slower now, eventually passing the horrible maisonette, which was on the far side of the water. In the residents' car park was a skip half full of rubble: the walls they'd already knocked through. Our work was raising the value of their portfolio.

Afterwards, I volunteered to wash our T-shirts and vests, enjoying the sour stench of them in my arms as I walked home.

While the clothes were on a hot cycle, I plugged in my tag to charge. I was just one of the appliances now. White goods.

Garthene texted to say: *Out with work. Back after curfew.*

All kisses withheld.

I hung the clothes on the drying horse in the lounge. I wanted to wait for her to return and see the flayed, fluorescent skins of guilty, repentant men. But it had been the first real day's work of my pitiful life and I fell asleep on the sofa and woke alone, my lower back throbbing, the vests glowing in the dark of the lounge, the words repeating around me, *Community Payback*, *Community Payback*, *Community Payback*.

I saw Garthene the next morning. I was up early, charging myself again. I'd chosen a plug socket by the kettle, bread bin and toaster, just to give me some breakfast options. She stood in the bedroom door in a stretched white T-shirt and boxer briefs.

'Husband 2.0, at your service,' I said.

She entered the room but stayed beyond the reach of my leash, her eyes on my ankle.

'What would you like to eat?' I said. 'I can make you anything so long as it's dry toast.' I made a joke of reaching for the butter dish, showing how it was just beyond my range of movement.

'How was community service?' she said.

'They call it payback now. And fine, actually. Good people. Very diverse.'

She nodded. 'What did you do?'

'Cleared brambles from the towpath.'

'Right.'

I took a half step towards her, stretching the cable taut. 'But can I make you something?'

'I think I'll eat at work.'

We used to joke that the hospital canteen was only for doctors who envied their patients' proximity to death.

'Okay,' I said.

She glanced again at my plugged-in leg. 'How long do you have to wear that, again?'

'Not too long. Eight months. I'll be the ultimate stay-at-home dad,' I said. 'By order of the Crown Prosecution Service.'

She chuckled without attaining actual amusement. Then she went to work.

While I finished charging, I drank a whole cafetière of coffee. I liked the way strong coffee introduced anxiety to everyday things, made opening innocuous letters suddenly frantic and crucial and, by the same token, could turn an already worrying situation into something truly terrifying.

My heart was hammering in my chest as I sat down at the dining table, opened my laptop and proceeded to very quickly produce eight extraordinarily forgettable tech news stories. I was not too proud to cannibalize week-old posts from ZDNet and Gizmodo and Gigaom and relaunch them in lumps of joyless prose. Such headlines as 'Five Questions to Help CIOs Avoid IoT Data Problems'. During my twenties I imagined my future life more beautiful, more creative, more profound than this. Back then, I had enjoyed boring, badly paid work because I could imagine telling future interviewers about it in the context of my brilliant success.

Once the eight articles were published, I did not track their popularity, as I used to. I did not spend hours refreshing lists of most viewed, most commented on, most shared, did not watch my rankings shift in real time, feeling proud and simultaneously disgusted that a thousand people would waste precious minutes of their life finding out how 'Pentaho Drives Blended BI'.

Instead I cleaned the toilet, something I had never done before. I had dabbed a little with the brush, but in all my thirty-three years had not spent one moment kneeling there with a scouring pad. Garthene spent a lot of time on the toilet these days, since her internal organs were being crushed against her pelvis by a tiny human, and this was for her.

I bleached the discoloured crust beneath the waterline, then scrubbed and scrubbed, creating a small vortex in the bowl so that spots of water flew up and hit my mouth and nose. Faeces and limescale and bleach. I wiped my face with my sleeve and carried on scrubbing as the insides of my nostrils wonderfully burned.

Garthene came in from work at eight. Her shift finished at five. It took twenty minutes to walk home, at most. I was not in a position to ask about the missing two hours and forty. She had either been saving a human life or making love to a colleague. She went straight to the toilet and, as she pissed, I listened. Once upon a time she might have left the door open. Once upon a time she might not have flushed, so that I could add my piss to hers, save water.

'Why is it clean in here?' she said.

'Because I love you.'

She stayed in the toilet in silence. There was no sink in there, no mirror, no books. Her phone was on the dining table.

The next day I received an email from a fellow tech journalist, Sam Lloyd. The subject line was *the world has finally noticed your talent* and the message contained a screen grab of the top ten most viewed stories on techtracker.co.uk. They were all written by me, covering various subjects, ranging from the low attendance at the 2010 XE Conference through to the mythical data speeds of 4G. The most popular story of all was one I'd written the previous year, when I still had the energy for being subversive:

> The Co-Star tablet comes at a mid-market price but with the processor and build of a – WAKE UP – far more boutique machine. The 8" Crystallic display reduces eye-strain and the – WAKE UP – projection keyboard keeps it feather-light. While the iPad may be more handsome to look at – RUN OUTSIDE – the Co-Star makes everything around you beautiful with – IT IS ALMOST CERTAINLY SUNNY – its TrueZoom lens, even in low light. There's no other tablet on – AND EARTH IS THE ONLY KNOWN PLANET WITH A BREATH-ABLE ATMOSPHERE – sale that can compete with the – GO! RUN! BREATHE! – Co-Star for value.

I couldn't help feeling, even now, that it was a pretty great piece of writing. And a part of me wasn't surprised that it had already been shared eight hundred plus times and there were a hundred and ninety-two new comments. I refreshed. Two hundred and six new comments. Two hundred and thirteen. I sat there, left-clicking, filling mostly with euphoria, just this tiny grape of discomfort lodged inside my chest. Over nine hundred shares. *Shares* was a nice word, redolent of human kindness and finance.

I never normally read the bottom half of the Internet, but I figured it might be interesting just to quickly browse down the length of the comments on my article, not to take in any particular words, but to feel the texture of the debate, the mood of the crowd, as though peering into a pub window during a football match.

I scrolled down rapidly, watching the comments rattle by, most of them short, one or two a little longer with patches of full capitals, and I kept going until I was safely among the sponsored links. It was hard not to read capitals even when they passed at great speed. A fragment stayed with me.

IF I SEE HIM IN THE STREET I WILL

I reassured myself that this sentence could end in all sorts of good ways.

I clicked Refresh. Two hundred and sixty-three comments. The shares were no longer measured by a specific number but had achieved abbreviation: 1.1k. I put my hand to my chest and rubbed my breastbone. The little grape inside me had grown to a lemon now, throbbing beneath my lungs.

I thought of how our obstetrician had showed us a poster on which brightly coloured fruits and vegetables glowed in sequence, to indicate the baby's development. It was nice to be infantilized.

I became aware that my phone was buzzing, had been buzzing.

It was on silent but was vibrating consistently on the kitchen counter, making a snoring sound. I watched it shuffle to the edge. There was a slight camber to the surface and the phone traversed the lip, knocked against a ramekin of sea salt, then made its way back inland.

My computer played a bugle call. That was my new mail sound. I had chosen it to remind myself that my joyless work had valour; historically, a *free lance* was a mercenary employed to wield rough justice among the lower orders. Then there was another bugle call – more mail – and then another and another, each new bugle interrupting the one before it, so that it no longer sounded heroic, or even like a bugle, just a single note, a flat line. I pressed Mute and, instead, watched the number of unread emails tick upwards. I tried to think of the ways in which the messages might be good news. Offers of work. Friend requests.

I refreshed the article. This time it was not found. I clicked through to my profile, but it didn't exist any more either. My photo had been deleted from the contributors page. I stood up and looked at my phone. I did not have a big social media presence, but the screen was now flowing with activity. A waterfall of mentions dropping away into the darkness, moving too fast to read.

'Looks like my review hit a nerve,' I said, out loud, to see if it sounded convincing.

There was a melon in my chest where the lemon had been.

I wrote *Raymond Morris good news* into the search bar.

I clicked *I'm feeling lucky*.

The screen filled with the image from the billboard truck: the one where I'm smiling.

The Sun's front page had that same picture with the headline 'Havin' a Riot Laugh'. The *Mirror* went with 'What a Riot'. The

Daily Sport cropped the image to just my face – with the caption 'Why Is This Pillock Happy? Find out on pages 8–9' – then ran the full image inside with a sidebar interview of the hardware store's owner:

> *What do you think of people who stood by smiling while*
> *   your life was destroyed?*
> *Mostly I feel sad for them.*

All the newspapers used the same photo, which showed the owner sitting on the edge of the pavement with his head in his hands, behind him the smashed window of his uninsured business of thirty-five years, while in the foreground I am happily receiving two cans of lager, dressed for a picnic. Three broadsheets ran the uncropped image across a double-page spread. Many of the articles mentioned my parents. How they owned a five-bedroom converted windmill. How my father had worked in insurance before retiring at fifty-five to volunteer at the lottery-funded Suffolk Festival. How my mother sold her art online, up to five hundred pounds for the biggest, saddest skies.

If you search for *Happy Tragedy Man* you will see where some jokers have Photoshopped me into various historical atrocities. There I am, smiling at Hiroshima. There I am, smiling as the towers burn. There I am, smiling in the village of Son My.

I know it's not my place to quibble, but the photo does not actually show me smiling *at* the destruction of the hardware shop. In fact I have turned away from the scene; I am facing the camera and so, in a sense, am *rejecting* voyeurism, smiling ruefully at the photographer's willingness to monetize other people's trauma. But attempts to interrogate photographic realism do not go well in the online comments.

The photographer's name was Burt Linden and this was by far his most successful image, published on every continent. He was interviewed about it on protophoto.net: 'Only when I got home and started going through the images on my laptop did I know I had something special.' I sent him a message through his website (subject line: I feel special?) but got an automated reply:

I'm away in Cuba until the end of the month so will be slow on emails. x

On a website called funjustice.com they listed my personal details: postcode, email, phone number, next of kin, links to articles, contact details of my employers. I received numerous text messages along the lines of *WHAT ARE YOU SMILING ABOUT, YOU TERRIBLE CUNT*. Many of these messages came from fellow iPhone users, I knew, because the messages turned blue. My work account stopped accepting new mail after the first thousand. Subjects included *i will find you*. All caps or no caps, those were the ones to watch out for. The take-home was that they hated my face. The shape of it, the piggy eyes, the noncommittal chin, the smug clean teeth. They hated the way I drank my beer, wrist kinked at the worst conceivable angle. The spotty shirt. They hated shorts, in general, and my shorts, specifically. Pop socks, which were a badge of evil. Tennis shoes not designed for actual tennis.

Garthene came in late again, this time carrying a large box. I was sitting at the dining table, my phone off, laptop open, taking a break from the messages of hate to luxuriate in some Pizza Express promotional emails, reading right through to the terms and conditions. She handed over the box then sat on the Swiss ball and stared at me.

'I guess you've seen the news,' I said.

Garthene practised what our midwife called an organizing breath. 'I have,' she said. 'And your parents keep calling me.'

'What do they want?'

'To speak to you. Because journalists are outside their house.'

'Oh God.'

I looked at the box in my hands. It was addressed to me in careful black marker, all caps. The sticker on the front listed the item as a gift and said *This Way Up*. I tried to believe that it contained nothing terrible, just a doughnut selection from a worried friend.

'Are you going to open it?' she said.

I gave it a gentle shake, trying to gauge its weight. 'Why wouldn't I?' I said.

The black electrical tape squealed as I tore it off. Garthene stood up from the Swiss ball. As I pulled open the flaps and peered inside, the smell came to us at once, the smell which had obviously been contained by the airtight seal, gaining weight in the heat of the delivery van, brewing in the glorious weather. I knew then, on some instinctive level, in the part of my simian brain attuned to marking territory, that this was the waste output of a fellow human, a human who hated me, a human who had gone to the trouble of discovering my address and producing a special bowel surge just for me, paying the little extra to track delivery so they could know in real time when the gift had reached its destination. Their personal ragu slid around the box, which they had sealed with pale blue tarpaulin to ensure a strong visual contrast and no leakage in transit. Whether they had deliberately avoided fibre or if it was just a lucky coincidence, I couldn't say. It wasn't until then that I understood, physically, what it meant to be despised. Because, for all the cruel emails and comments, for the messages from editors explaining they could not use me again, for the knowledge that banks and insurers and mortgage brokers considered me an unsafe risk, for the fact that the Internet would remember my shame for ever, I still didn't really comprehend the world's resentment until tiny faecal particles entered my lungs and, therefore, bloodstream, until my nose and mouth were bathed in that stench, until I could taste it, at which point I immediately knelt and vomited into the recycling bin, a petite ball of yellowish bile pooling in an empty egg box. The smell of my own insides was, in this context, a huge relief. Garthene was at the window now, her head right outside. She looked like she was ready to jump.

We both agreed Garthene would be better off staying at Marie and Lee's with the twenty-four-hour security. Better for me to face these troubles alone. Once she was safely out of the flat, I pressed a balled-up tea towel over my nose and mouth while I took photos of the faeces with my phone, one with flash, one with natural light. Then I resealed the box – triple-gaffered it – carried it out to the bus stop and waited for the 488. I had time to examine the postmark and address. Whoever had sent this had very neat handwriting.

When I got to the police station, I was disappointed to find that neither Dana nor Liam was working reception. Instead, there was a pale young officer who had a concentrated patch of freckles across his nose, so that his face resembled a sneeze-filled tissue.

'Is Dana around?' I said.

'What's it regarding?'

'I'd like to speak to her about something.'

'What something?'

The box was at my feet. 'A private matter.'

'Fine. Name, please?'

I told him and immediately regretted it. He was clearly a tabloid man and I could see the cheap headlines running behind his eyes.

'Oh, in *that* case,' he said, rolling his seat back.

He was away for longer than necessary, then the side door opened and she was there.

'Hi again, Mr Morris. How can I help you?'

She made me leave the box in a cupboard – she didn't touch it – and then we walked through an office. Three men at three desks pretended to be working, but each individually glanced up over their partitions as I passed. Dana took me to a meeting room. We sat in padded blue chairs around a circular table. I slid my phone across the desk. She peered down at the photo. She did not touch the screen.

'I see,' she said.

'Look at the next one. It's even worse with the flash on.'

With the nail of her index finger, she pushed the phone back towards me.

'The thing is, Dana, I can handle the abusive messages, but this . . . My wife doesn't feel safe.'

'The thing is, Ray, it's actually not that unusual for someone in your situation to get the odd nasty delivery. If it's any comfort, it only tends to last a week or two.'

'Okay but shouldn't you at least call the lab, run the DNA?'

She gave me a small smile. My knowledge of police procedure was endearing. 'We *could* do that, but we have to weigh up costs. It's expensive to get a decent sample, particularly from faeces, and then we'd need to build a case, which again costs money, and I'm not sure my boss would give it the go-ahead.'

'*You* should be the boss,' I said, trying to get our old banter going.

'You're right. I should be,' she said. She hadn't even got out her notepad. 'In my experience, the people who do this sort of thing aren't violent.' Dana shrugged.

'Dana, did you just shrug? Is this a shrug-level alert for you?'

She leaned across and touched my shoulder twice with the middle of her palm. Pat and then, also, pat. 'Keep that sense of humour,' she said. She stood and opened the door.

She made me take the box away.

It was clear that the only way I could respond to these attacks was to be the bigger man, the biggest. So I bravely worked through my hate mail. I apologized to each message, never copy-pasting from one to the next, always typing bespoke, which seemed crucial.

Dear Sir, I completely understand your anger but let me say that my smile was not in response to the shopkeeper's misfortune . . .

Dear Madam, I was actually not privately educated but I take your point . . .

Dear Ms, I agree that my lenient treatment in court was, in large part, due to the colour of my skin, and I'd be happy to support any awareness-raising . . .

I killed them with kindness, really murdered them with it.

Dan sent us a message explaining that, after recent events, he no longer felt able to represent us in our 'search for a home'. To be dumped by an estate agent. On top of that, he explained that our current landlord was receiving emails that were very negative about me – as a tenant, as a human – and he was terminating my contract due to antisocial behaviour. That gave us one month to pack up and move out. The only upside to everything going terribly in my life was that bad news like this – traumas that would ordinarily have seemed disastrous: sudden eviction from our home – were almost forgettable in the context of my wider absolute oblivion.

I received an airmailed death threat written with highlighter pens. I also received a letter of support saying these people shouldn't be allowed to own shops in our country.

Reddit detectives quickly assembled a cache of images of me during the disturbances. I was wearing such easily identifiable clothes. They found a phone video of me outside the town hall, working my house key into the palm of my hand. The one benefit of this video was that some people then suggested I needed clinical help and that took some of the heat off.

My biggest fear was that an Internet lunatic would track down Garthene. I received Google alerts whenever someone on the web used her name. This was distressing because, up until then, she had had almost no online presence. Searching for *Garthene Henderson* used to locate just the one article she wrote at nineteen years old while on unlikely work experience with UEFA.co.uk. A thoughtful piece about changes to the seeding criteria for the qualifying rounds of the Europa League. Even *Garthene* on its own offered only 2,105 hits, mostly new cemetery listings from the American South. It was clear that there had once been a generation of Garthenes but they were dying fast. *Garthene Dickson, Mount Hope Cemetery, Bangor, USA, 1926 to 2011*. It used to make me happy to think that soon my wife would be the last one carrying the burden. I used to text her: *Your tribe lost another elder*. But now her name was multiplying in the jokily evil and evilly jokey depths of Reddit. *Let's set up a Kickstarter to pay for Garthene's divorce lawyer, who's with me?*

I called her every two hours.

'I'm alive,' she said.

'Just checking.'

Then, on the afternoon of the second day, she didn't answer. I texted but got no response. I let that go and, two hours later, called again. Voicemail said her phone was *unreachable*. I waited ten minutes and called again. Then I waited no minutes and called again. Marie and Lee were on a twelve-day trip to Kyoto, reliving one of their formative holidays, so Garthene was alone in their house and, it seemed immediately clear, had been murdered by vigilante justice-bringers from the dark web. I left the flat and ran. Running through the streets was normal for me now.

When I got to Marie and Lee's, Yuku did not open the gate. He put his hand on my shoulder.

'Have any weirdos tried to get in?' I said.

'You're the first one.'

'I just need to see her.' I held on to the bars of the gate and called her name.

'Get some sleep,' Yuku said.

I ignored him and started to climb, wedging my right foot into the ornate swirls. He yanked me down to the tarmac and rested his weight on me, knelt on my arms. What impressed me most was that he managed to pin me to the floor while still giving the clear impression that he didn't want to, that he felt sympathy for my situation, and it was only his professionalism crushing the air from my lungs.

'You're okay,' he said. 'And so is she.'

When I looked across I could see Garthene, completely alive, watching at the window.

The next time I saw her in the flesh was at the hospital. Jenny called us in for an extra scan because the placenta was still too low, probably because of how I had ruined our lives. Garthene was bigger now, a hint of the cowboy walk as she moved across the car park.

'You look fantastic,' I said.

'I'm a beast.'

'A fantastic beast,' I said.

I was wearing my most generic adult clothes: navy shirt, straight jeans, shoes that resisted description. They were just shoes.

She observed my new maturity. 'Are you okay?'

'I'm improving.'

'Have you been sleeping?'

'Not if I can avoid it.'

'I can get you some pills.'

Her kindness was unsettling. It occurred to me that she agreed with those on the Internet who thought I was mentally ill.

'What are those?' she said, looking down.

'I call them shoes.'

In the low-lit room, she sat in a special reclining seat, the young female sonographer took a chair on wheels, and there was an inanimate one for me. Garthene pulled her T-shirt up over her bump. The tube of conductive gel farted as the technician squirted it on, which I found not at all funny on the assumption that both the sonographer and my wife were far beyond finding anything in the hospital rude or amusing.

The young sonographer barked with laughter and said: 'Ex*cuse* me.'

On the screen, our creature emerged, squirming in a pool of static, showing off its insides. I watched the sonographer jab the device into Garthene's pelvis.

'Placenta's risen slightly but it's still low,' she said. 'We'll have to wait and see on that one. Do you want to know the sex?'

I turned to Garthene. Her body, her choice. Months ago we had agreed that we wanted the sex to be a surprise because, in our privileged lives, there was so little beyond our control and wouldn't it be exhilarating for just one moment to feel utterly dazed and adrift.

'I was thinking it might be quite good to find out,' she said.

'Absolutely,' I said.

'One less thing to think about.'

'Of course.'

The sonographer nodded and started scanning again. 'Okay then, let's see.'

It did not take long. On the screen we saw what looked, at first, like a tiny brain resolve itself unmistakably into a pair of testicles, the fractal walnut of a ball sack. And like that, a whole timeline fell away. All our intelligent, beautiful daughters, their sarcasm at breakfast, were gone. Goodbye Lily, goodbye Nancy, goodbye Ruby. In their place, the blocky monosyllables – Dave, Tom, Rob – thinking with their nuts. I hadn't realized how badly I wanted a girl until then. I was sure that Garthene felt the same, but I had not seen her in some time and I wanted to make this moment positive.

'Did you see those beauties?' I said.

'I did,' she said. 'King cojones!'

She was also trying to be upbeat.

'Ha ha ha,' I said. It felt good to celebrate together, even if neither of us meant it.

'The massive balls of a champion,' she said.

It was only now, hearing her make basic jokes, that I realized how long it had been since I'd seen her enjoy herself. My dumb behaviour over the last few weeks had forced her into being the grown-up one, and it was great to be reminded of the childishness I fell in love with.

Garthene cleaned the conductive gel off with two tissues, one to wipe, one to polish. Out in the waiting room, I put my lips against her neck and kissed the charming, harmless mole she has there. She didn't fully reciprocate but did rub my back. She didn't hate me, that was clear. She something else'd me, but I did not know what.

As we made our way slowly back through the corridors, blinking beneath the box lights, Garthene got out her phone and started texting. I watched a small, private smile gain weight on her face. I recognized it, the smile of someone trying not to, which is the worst one. She caught me looking at it, the smile, and banished it to her eyes.

I allowed myself to glance at her screen. There were three small words which I couldn't read, then a couple of kisses. Knowing she reserved *xx* for expressions of true and lasting love, it would have been easy for me to become jealous. But I wasn't that person any more and so I decided it was probably just hormones allowing her to *xx* more freely. Or perhaps the *xx* were not kisses but XX chromosomes and she was just texting a colleague the news of our child's sex. That latter thought had a lovely shape and it was the one I decided to believe as I walked slowly over the linoleum, keeping pace with my wife, enjoying the way the corridor mellowly replicated itself.

But then, as we passed by the Diabetes Centre, I had a challenging thought.

Is XX a girl or a boy?

Instinctively you'd think XY was female because it has a girly ending, though the idea of endings being gendered was exactly the kind of horseshit I would not be passing on to my boy. Garthene's phone buzzed in her hand. The person had replied straight away and, as she read the message, the private smile came back for a curtain call.

'Who're you texting?' I said.

'A friend,' she said.

'Your boyfriend?' I said, giving her the chance to run with a joke.

'He's not my boyfriend,' she said.

That did not feel good.

'Bet he's handsome though?' I said, giving her another opportunity.

She put the phone in her pocket.

That meant I had to look up XX on my phone and learn it meant female, not male, and this meant she was texting kisses, not chromosomes, and that meant, with sincere regret, that I would have to stalk her.

The next day I wore jogging bottoms and a black NYC baseball cap – clothes that would make me invisible to Garthene – while I waited at the bus stop near the hospital staff exit. She emerged a little after five, used the handrail to descend the three steps to the car park, then headed south-east, walking slowly with her legs wide, her bump entering sunlight before her. There were no cars, but she waited for the beeps before crossing the road.

Resting on a bench by the war memorial, she received another smile-inducing text. In all honesty, I didn't really think she was having an affair but, by *acting* as though she was, I could allow us both to experience the texture of my melodramatic actions. That way we could enjoy discovering how madly I loved her, how my love was a sickness, how I was crazy from loneliness and jealousy, all without the time-consuming rigmarole of having her actually fuck around.

I knelt in the bandstand beside a street-sleeper who was not sleeping. The flagstone beneath him was a darker colour and worn smooth. While I watched Garthene, the street-sleeper watched me and I felt I needed to justify myself.

'I think she's having an affair,' I said.

He squinted at her. 'It's not an affair if she's not your wife.'

'She *is* my wife,' I said.

He looked at my face, then at my NYC cap, then at the bulge of my ankle tag. I emptied the coin section of my wallet on to his sleeping bag. He counted the silvers and golds and examined the two-euro coin.

'Okay,' he said. 'Now you're married.'

Garthene got up and I followed her all the way to Marie and Lee's place where Yuku saluted her and opened the gate while I hid in a phone box. Soon there will be no phone boxes left and where will all the creepy people go?

The second day, I started packing up our stuff and putting our books into boxes, pausing to flick through the photo album from our wedding day. The best image was of us laughing at the vows.

I spent the afternoon sitting at the bus stop. I watched the smoke rise from the hospital incinerator: tumours and appendices. You're not allowed to keep them, even if you want to. When Garthene came out she walked the same route, stopped on the same bench, but this time made friends with a young woman's tiny dog, a mini sausage, holding its paws in her hands, doing a little rock 'n' roll dancing. I mention this only because even the Garthene I fell in love with – fun-time Garthene – still despised tiny dogs and their owners and, most of all, fools who would crouch in the street and indulge them. But she was more open these days.

The street-sleeper said: 'That is a damn cute dog.'

I explained how inbreeding for cuteness causes untold health problems. Pugs can't breathe through their adorable faces. Harnesses keep their eyeballs in.

He shook his head. 'Don't be like that,' he said.

I went home and continued to clear out the flat and my inbox. Behind the bed, I collected a handful of fluorescent ear plugs that must have fallen from Garthene's ears in the night.

Day three, no sign of Garthene. I stayed sitting at the bus stop and got sunburned. On a nearby bench, two blue-gowned inpatients smoked and ate boneless popcorn chicken, their IVs beside them on wheelie stands. I liked the look of the chicken and they saw that in my eyes. I'd been awake most of the night, apologizing, and was constantly hungry for yellow food. One of the men held out his paper box and shook it. I picked up a lump and gobbled it down. That's one great thing about being an unusual person. All the other unusuals are totally on your side.

Across the road was the Hospital Tavern, a pub prized for an older clientele who all seemed in some comforting way to have made terrible choices in their lives. It had red-tinted windows and a grey parrot in a cage and it was not unusual for Jean, the landlady, to ring the last orders bell then yell, 'I'm pretending it's last orders,' which was thrilling, though it was important not to appear thrilled.

Garthene and I used to call it the Scary Arms because one of the regulars wore sleeveless vests to show off the scars up the insides of his wrists, home-made tattoos distorted through the thickened flesh. He wore decorative hospital tags on both wrists. He was out there now, smoking a Superking.

'You've been waiting for that bus for days,' he yelled to me. 'Where are you going?'

'Nowhere,' I said.

A bus was coming. It stopped and the doors hissed back. From my seat, I asked the lady driver if she was going nowhere and she said Leytonstone and I said no thanks. It was exhilarating to make Scary Arms laugh.

Day four, I went up into the attic. The air made me feel like I was breathing through a pillow. In the half-light, I could make out the shapes of our discarded dreams: Garthene's pedal-powered pottery wheel; my five-octave Roland with keys weighted for a more nuanced, emotional performance; evidence of the shameful summer we thought we might get into kiteboarding. I tried to remember what kind of people we were when we bought a tin of beeswax and a swatch of corduroy to keep our real-leather walking boots supple. At the far end of the space, I saw our neighbours' workbench, touring bike and valve amplifier – different dreams, different failures. In every direction, the ceilings angled down.

I went out to my bus stop and waited for Garthene, followed her to Marie and Lee's. She stopped at my street-sleeper, made him laugh then gave him a ten-pound note.

Day five. All our belongings were packed and labelled and I'd reached the moment I'd been dreading: inbox zero. I had run out of people to be sorry to. I defrosted the freezer and cleaned the fridge. I never realized you could drink the liquid in the pouches of mozzarella.

I was two hours early for the end of Garthene's shift, so I went into the Hospital Tavern and asked for the smallest drink. Jean gave me sambuca. Her hair was dyed a coppery red and so was her scalp. I sipped my sambuca and went to the window, rapped my knuckles on the sill.

'Who're you looking for?' Jean said.

'My wife.'

'Ex- or future?' she said.

'Ha ha.'

Scary Arms was the only other person in the pub. He was playing Millionaire and occasionally yelling out questions. 'It's called the fontanelle!' I said, excited to know the answer to something, my voice suddenly loud. He won twenty quid and bought me another sambuca, this one in a tumbler. It was my drink now. My usual.

When Garthene came out of the hospital I'd had six usuals and my teeth were woolly. She stood in the car park and phoned someone. They answered immediately and she angled her face to the sunshine. If she had then walked south-east, back towards Marie and Lee's, I might have left her alone, stayed with my new good friends, finished my seventh usual, but she didn't. She sat down at my bus stop. Gary and Jean came to the window. Scary Arms's real name was Gary. I knew that now.

'There goes your *wife*,' he said, raising his hands to make air quotes, scar tissue flexing.

Garthene got on a single-decker W15 and I caught the one after it, a few minutes later. In London, you know you're going nowhere good if the bus has just one deck. There was bad traffic and I could still see Garthene's bus about fifteen vehicles ahead. I stayed stand-ing at the front, next to the driver, watching the road, leaning on the perforated Plexiglas screen. That's where the unusual people always stand. I knew that we had a good chance of catching her because, if you think about it, the bus in front acts as a kind of snowplough, clearing away all the passengers so that the bus behind makes ground. That's why three buses coming at once is not bad luck but cold logic.

It was a low-speed chase. Both buses stopped at a long light. Her bus squeezed through on a yellow which was red by the time we got there, but my driver pushed on anyway and I said out loud, 'Yes, great driving.' If you've never been the bus's unusual person then you're missing out.

Garthene got off on Leyton High Road. We both did. Dan, our estate agent, had always told us this was a surprisingly nice part of town and we'd always said we'd rather die. I tracked Garthene down the high street. All the shop signs had been hand-painted on wooden backboards, including *Kebabish* and *Send Money International*. She turned on to an uglier road of two-storey new builds, a badly fitted paving slab gulping as she stepped on it. I followed, hopping over the loose stone. The houses on this north-facing side of the street had few and tiny windows, presum-ably to improve energy efficiency, though the impression was dystopian, expanses of orange brick interrupted by mean little peepholes. Garthene stopped at a plastic door. Parked outside was a blue Vauxhall Astra, the same car that had dropped her home the night I got out of jail. *The night I got out of jail.* I had such sentences inside me.

She rang the bell and got buzzed in. I followed up to the door and let my finger rest on the bell. The important thing, I reminded

myself, was not whether she *had* betrayed me but that she understand what actions I would take if she *did*. So it was vital I *believed*
the worst was happening, that she and some ex-patient whose
muscle density was just returning were exploring each other's
bodies in an adult softplay room, exuberantly lubricated, coded
messages of affection passing back and forth between non-
biological father's penis and unborn child, like two prisoners
knocking on the pipes. I hovered my finger over the bell's rubbery
button. I pressed the bit of door frame next to the bell a few times,
to get a feel for it.

I thought of Lee coming around his marital bed on all fours with
another man's used condom hanging in his jaws. As a direct result
of his unstable behaviour, he and Marie were now back together,
walking through Japanese moss gardens. They would probably
soon be trying for a baby. *Trying* for a baby, as though it would be
a chore for the two best-looking people I know to bring each other
to nightly, bareback orgasm.

I lowered my finger to touch the subtly ribbed button but didn't
press.

You need to be drunk to make this kind of thing work. I tried
to channel my six drinks, locate my inner sambucas. I pressed the
button, held it. Above me, a soft sound of Christmas bells.

'Hello?'

'This is Ray.'

'Ray?'

'Yes, Ray,' I said. 'Garthene's husband.'

'Oh, Ray, it's nice to fina—'

'Open the fucking door.'

Swearing is always a risk with a voice like mine, but I felt like
it landed.

The bolt buzzed back. 'I'm at the top.'

I stomped up the carpeted stairs, two at a time, sliding my palm along the textured wallpaper, trying to remain out of control. This man knew who I was, probably because they had been saying my name, speaking of the devil, to intensify the sex act. They had summoned me. That was their fetish.

On the carpet running up the stairs, there was a trail of dots, bin-juice stains, that led directly to the feet of the man standing on the landing. He was very tall – six foot four or five – right on the boundary between commanding and absurd, and I imagined he could tip himself either way, depending on his shoes. In this instance, brown loafers with goaty little tassels. I recognized him. I'd seen him at the hospital. It was her colleague, the pillow-lender.

'I'm Peter,' he said.

He offered me his hand but I didn't want it. I went straight past him and inside the flat, where Garthene was leaning against the round dining table with all her clothes on. She was holding a mug of what appeared to be bag-in herbal tea. I looked around the room for something to react against. There was a frosted-glass screen that tried to suggest the kitchen area was a separate room from the living area but convinced no one. On the fridge-freezer was a microwave and on the microwave a kettle. The quality of the handles on the cupboards was dreadful. The only thing that was arguably a betrayal was the slightly burnt lasagne in a large oven dish on the counter. He was feeding her, feeding my wife her death-row meal. That was a start. I saw a small camp bed set up in one corner of the room. I went over and sat on it, bounced on the mattress a little, just for the evocative sound of the springs.

'Oh, I see,' I said. 'Came here for a quick sleep break, did you?'

Peter was now standing in a corner of the kitchen area,

head slightly bowed, fingers threaded around a mug in front of his stomach. I sensed he was trying not to look physically intimidating, which was, in its own way, physically intimidating. There were cards on top of the television. One of them said: *Happy 40th*.

Garthene said: 'Peter and I were just having a chat.'

'I bet you were,' I said. 'Deciding on a safe word.'

Garthene and Peter looked at each other, then he slid along the counter and opened the front door. 'I get the feeling it'd be easier if I gave you two space,' he said. 'So I'll just be out on the landing.'

The door shut very gently. His exit took something away from me and I was unable to continue my baseless accusations. Garthene was now sitting, staring at her hands, her legs set wide and geezery.

'How did you get here?' she said.

'I've been following you.'

'Oh God,' she said. 'Ray, you should try talking to someone. You might find it helpful.'

'Lovely,' I said. 'Because a problem shared is a problem halved.'

'It is.'

'And then you share your genitals.'

She rubbed her right eye with her knuckles.

'What do you and him even talk about?' I said.

'Anything.'

'About how your husband has no job, no prospects, will never own a home, how people in the street despise him.'

'Sometimes.'

'Great,' I said, and I stood up. I began to pace, trying to build momentum. 'I bet Peter can really listen. I bet he makes you feel *heard*.' I said this loud enough for him to hear outside.

'Take it easy.'

'All hail the male nurse!' The room was so small it required a neat turning circle. 'Kindness upon kindness! Sweet Peter, never judging, always sensitive to difference.' I picked up speed. 'I bet he's never crossed a line in his whole –'

'Shut-up-Ray. Just shut up.'

There was a tremor in her voice I was a little surprised to hear. She covered her eyes with one hand. Her mouth-breathing became audible. I hoped that Peter might choose this moment to step inside and ask me politely to leave, let me wrestle him a little and throw a punch, have Garthene hold me back. But there was no sign of him, which was disappointing. I went over and opened the door, looked out into the dark communal space with bike-wheel scuff marks on the walls, a smell of drains.

'That was your cue to step in, old boy,' I said. 'I'm making your guest uncomfortable.'

He wasn't even waiting to come in. He was sitting on the top step with both of his thoughtful hands over his mouth, staring directly ahead. I watched him for a moment, let the door close on its own weight, then turned back to Garthene, who still had her eyes covered. They were both covering up bits of their body. There was an atmosphere in the room that someone who'd drunk fewer sambucas might have been alert to.

'Just for clarity,' I said, 'you're upset because of my wild-man behaviour, right? There's no subtext I'm missing?' I looked around the flat. 'I only ask because I thought Peter might have intervened by now. That feels like something he would do.' I went and opened the door again. He was still out there, unmoving, both hands at his mouth. 'Now's your chance,' I told him.

He didn't move.

It was one of those modern homes that was so well insulated, when the door fell shut it felt like the room held its breath.

Garthene stood and walked to the sink.

'Now's the moment when you tell me that I've got it completely wrong,' I said. '*Ray, you've gone crazy*. That sort of thing. *I'm worried about you, Ray, have you been drinking?*'

'We'll get through this,' she said.

'Get through what?' I said.

She held on to the kitchen counter with both hands.

'I have been drinking, by the way, so that would explain why I seem a bit out there.'

'We'll get through this.' She said it again.

'Get through what?' I said. 'Are you going to make me guess?'

I stood directly behind her as she observed the plughole.

'Okay, first try. Let's get the obvious one out the way. Have you two slept together?'

There seemed to be something of great interest in the sink.

'I've got other better guesses,' I said. 'That one's a total cliché.'

'Yes.'

'Yes, it's a cliché? Or yes, you've slept with him?'

'Yes, I've slept with him.'

It's possible not to hear a sentence, if you really concentrate. Even after you've heard it, you can go back and unhear it, if you really try. When she turned around to face me, her eyes were wet, but I don't think you would say she was crying. The wetness just saved her from having to see me.

'I'm sorry,' she said.

All my sambucas were with me now and I wasn't standing. At some point I'd crossed the room and sat back down on the small camp bed. She had changed from gripping the kitchen counter to gripping the back of a chair. There was a muffled noise from outside – a throat noise, presumably Peter's.

'Ray, I'm so sorry,' she said. 'We were drunk.'

'Of course you were,' I said. 'What did you drink? Sambuca?' That was an in-joke between me and myself.

'It only happened once,' she said.

'Only once?' I said, my voice suddenly loud. 'Why didn't you say so? Once is only one more than none.'

There were two reflective vertical strips on her cheeks. They flashed in the light as she turned to the window.

'I guess it happened right here,' I said. I prodded the pouffiest bit of duvet with my forefinger. I prodded it again, really worked a knuckle in. I was crying now too. What a loser.

'Where was I when you did it?' I said.

'Away.' Her voice was quiet.

'Away where?'

'At a conference.'

'Which conference?'

'In Bonn.'

'In Bonn!' I said, yelling it. 'So I was in the Rhineland!' I wanted to find a way to loudly say Rhineland again. 'If I was in the Rhineland that means it happened in January.'

I heard the floorboards creak as Peter's weight shifted in the corridor. I paused. There was a thought hovering above us. *January*. There was something special about January, but the sambuca was protecting me from it.

Peter was in the doorway now, his hands unclenched at his sides.

'And here he is,' I said, 'looking super virile.'

Garthene bowed her head, sobbing silently. Her mouth had strings of saliva in it and some of the saliva had come out on to her chin and it was sticky and white. She was dehydrated. It was infuriating to find that even now I could want to give her a glass of water. I rejected that instinct and, instead, rose to my feet and backhand-swiped her half-full mug off the table. It bounced three times on the linoleum, then landed upright, unharmed. It said *Save the NHS*.

PART FOUR

I moved into Dave's one-bedroom ex-local flat. He'd finally managed to buy his own place, thus joining Marie in the elite category of landowner. We stacked the boxes of my belongings two-deep and three-high in an L-shape in the corner of his lounge, creating for me what we called a private gated development. I slept on a blow-up mattress behind the walls of boxes. It was not at all a metaphor to say I was living in the shadow of what was left of my marriage.

Since I no longer had any paid work and mostly did not sleep, I had plenty of time to research Garthene's betrayal. January was the month in which we conceived a child. Or, to remove all uncertainty, January was the month in which *she* conceived a child. I examined the calendar on our fertility app. It showed that I was away in Bonn eight days before she ovulated. That meant that Peter's sperm would have needed to survive for over a week in order to fertilize my wife. This was, I discovered, possible.

On the family-planning forums of cleverstork.com and everythingmybabyknows.co.nz, there was much impassioned anecdotal evidence from people who said they had first-hand experience of it. In one scientific study, sperm had been kept alive in a test tube for ten days in an alkaline solution which was designed to imitate the environment created by the female orgasm. The bigger the orgasm the friendlier the habitat. Thus Peter bringing Garthene to climax – the kind of full-body screamer only attainable through condomless home-wrecking while the husband is away at a predictive analytics conference – would create the ideal conditions for his sperm to test the limits of human biology.

The whole debate was, of course, dependent on whether they had used a condom. I was certainly not going to ask Garthene or Peter for confirmation. I preferred to let both narratives exist simultaneously. Schrödinger's sheath. The more I thought about it, the no-condom narrative was actually *better* than its alternative. If there was no condom then at least you could say they were hammered and sloppy and did not think of anything but slamming their bare genitals together as quickly and as firmly as possible. Unprotected sex could be attributed to temporary mania. But if they *did* use a condom then that meant they had the time to think about it, had time to visualize me eating potato pancakes alone in the Bonn ibis, and still go ahead with it.

I lost touch with day and night. I read a fat book called *Expecting Everything*. I liked its cover, a picture of a non-idealized baby, a baby with blotchy skin. It had no chapter on ambiguous paternity, nothing on sperm survival rates in cervical fluid. Instead I worked through the huge section of alphabetized diseases. It was a relief to know that all birth defects would now be her fault because she had maintained a stressful lie throughout the child's uterine development.

I learned every disease off by heart. *AIDS*, *anencephaly*, *autism*, *biotinidase deficiency*. I found it helpful to quietly enunciate them. *Bronchiolitis*, *cerebral palsy*, *classic galactosemia*. I whispered to myself, '*classic* galactosemia'. After each disease, the book gave a figure, a likelihood: 1 in 2,000, 1 in 350, 1 in 100. I found myself hoping some children would take the brunt of maybe three or four serious conditions at once and cook the books a little. It was painful to concede that, even if the child was Peter's, I cared for it above other children. *Cleft lip, club foot, congenital heart defect.* Some diseases, I knew, were specific to certain ethnic groups. Tay-Sachs disease I sent up to Stamford Hill before wafting sickle-cell anaemia to Dalston. *Encephalopathy, Fabry disease, Gaucher disease.*

I also reread *Let Your Body Lead*, the hypnobirthing manual that Kamara had lent us back in April. Garthene had always said hypnobirthing was bullshit, and instinctively I agreed, but I was beginning to like the idea that pain could be a matter of opinion. If one renames contractions as surges or waves then they become no more fearful than any other bodily process and the birth occurs without fuss, the child slithering loose with the ecstatic rush of a sneeze. The book said some women even have orgasmic births where each wave produces a rush of the trust hormone oxytocin which, in turn, brings on another wave, which encourages more oxytocin, and so on, until the delivery room floods with good feelings, all previous grievances washed away as the baby surfs free on a trustgasm.

I got an email from Garthene in the middle of the night. It had been eleven days since our last contact, longer than the lifespan of even the most outdoorsy sperm. She told me she hoped I would still be present at the birth. She sent the message at 04.21, which meant she too couldn't sleep. I texted her immediately.

Can't sleep?

No.

Must be the awful things you've done.

There were the little dots which meant she was typing. I watched them for a while before her message came through: *Yes.* And then she added: *And I saw the sonographer again.*

And?

The placenta is still low. Looks like it's going to be a C-section.

It was a stretch to associate low placentas with low morals, but I was very limber.

I guess that's your fault. Along with everything else.

Okay.

Good. And where are you staying?

Marie's.

Every night or just some nights?

I watched the dots.

Every night. There was a pause. *So you'll be at the birth?*

I let her stew for a while. Seconds and seconds. *Yes, I'll be there.*

After that, I watched a lot of medical training videos of Caesarians on YouTube. My favourite one had a soundtrack of mellow jazz piano as four disembodied hands worked scalpels, needles, spreaders. Every minute or so, a subtitle floated past: *the Pfannenstiel incision . . . the right stay suture . . . inspecting the pouch of Douglas . . .* Halfway through the video, the hands ripped the wound wider. Apparently tears heal faster than incisions, though it looks medieval. You can hear it, too. A small creaking sound like a tiny door opening. In the comments underneath, someone called TrustMeImA talked about how the electrocauterizing device they use to reduce bleeding creates the smell of burning flesh. He said he used to find the smell distressing but slowly got used to it and now, if he's had a long shift and not eaten, it makes him salivate. *Barbecue is still barbecue*, he wrote. *The sweet scent of burning subcutaneous fat, like that of a sizzling strip steak.* I watched this video on loop, feeling my horror and revulsion reduce with each viewing until I was blissfully desensitized, only the soft diminished chords getting through.

15th September, 8.45 a.m. The operation was scheduled for ten and we arranged to meet an hour before, to talk things through. I got there early and sat in the too-bright coffee shop attached to the hospital's reception area. It had plastic wood-effect walls and groups of blank-eyed loved ones eating muffins without pleasure. I ordered a double espresso. That was one good thing about being very tired and very sad: strong coffee could not touch me now. Its only function was to give me something to blame my feelings on. What was that unshiftable inner hollowness? Must be the coffee.

After a few minutes, Garthene walked into reception. She was early too, wearing white trainers and an orange summer dress. She'd dressed up for her Caesarian. She looked around, didn't see me, checked her phone, glanced up at the strange sculpture of a metal fish hanging beneath the skylight, checked her phone again, walked in circles. She was nervous. We both were. I realized then that this meeting most closely resembled a first date. Except with the added pressure of guaranteed co-parenting.

She finally spotted me and waved. I was aware that the decision of whether to hug was mine. I got up and opened my arms. We came together and instantly knew it was a bad connection. Her belly was in the way and so we ended up kind of leaning over it to hug one another, which gave the whole thing a frigid politeness, as of awkward cousins at a memorial.

'How're you feeling?' I said.

'I'm actually really scared,' she said.

I don't know why that surprised me. Or why it made me feel good.

'I'm also scared,' I said.

'I'm terrified, actually,' she said. Her voice was thin.

'Well, it makes sense,' I said. 'This is all unbelievably frightening.'

Our first date was going well.

Our midwife, Jenny, was waiting for us at obstetrics.

'Showtime,' she said. She hugged us both.

She was wearing skate shoes and a fluorescent purple lanyard that had the word *MIDWIFE* in huge white capitals on it, the information presented with such aggressive clarity that it could only indicate our soon-to-be-degraded mental capacities.

'Let's get you changed,' Jenny said.

She showed me to a small room where I put on a green gown, little sheaths over my normal shoes and a shower cap over my hair. When I arrived at theatre, an older male doctor with visible blood vessels in his cheeks immediately shook my hand.

'I'm Dr Phil,' he said. 'I'll be operating today.'

'Nice to meet you.'

'You don't need to worry about your wife. For her, it'll just feel like someone's rummaging in her handbag.' He laughed at his own joke. Garthene didn't own handbags. He had no idea what kind of people we were. 'And have no fear, I'll keep it neat. *All* incisions below the bikini line.' He squeezed my shoulder. It was easy to imagine him posting YouTube comments under the name Trust-MeImA. *Barbecue is still barbecue.*

Garthene's body was divided along the line of her shoulders by a blue curtain. On one side was her head, with Jenny and me. On the other were her reproductive organs, lit by surgical lamps on ceiling-mounted cranes, and flanked by two obstetricians, Dr Phil and a female doctor, both gowned, gloved and masked.

'I know you weren't planning it to happen this way,' I said to Garthene's head, 'but at least we'll get to see baby sooner.'

'Thank you,' she said.

In some of the birth books aimed at fathers, they even suggest specific lines of comforting dialogue.

From behind the curtain, there came the chinking of tools. I had expected them to wait a while, to let us get in the zone. But, peering over into the spotlights, I saw the female doctor swab Garthene's midriff and paint it yellow, before the other one, Phil, made a horizontal incision about six inches long, then made a deeper incision along the same line, and then again, deeper, his eyes narrowing, slicing through fat and connective tissue. Much less blood than you'd expect. Hardly any.

'Ray?' Garthene said. 'It's rude to stare.'

Dr Phil said: 'No talking please,' and she made an oops face and gave a laugh and I realized the opiates had lowered her humour threshold. As they cut through the five layers of flesh, I patted her forehead with a handkerchief I had bought for this very moment. Then, from behind the curtain, there was a short creaking noise, and Garthene blew out air.

'Pain or just pressure?' Jenny said.

'Pressure,' she said.

I didn't mean to look but, once I did, there was no turning away. The wound was bigger now and Dr Phil was holding open the bottom of it with a stainless-steel device that resembled a shoehorn. The female doctor dabbed at a membrane with an electrical device that resembled a fountain pen and out came the watery blood. It had been there all along. That was followed by the smell of burning flesh. In my head, I introduced the soft jazz chords of medical-emotional detachment. But the smell got stronger as a twist of smoke rose from the wound. My only other mechanism for keeping calm was to take a deep breath, which I realized, too late, was counterproductive. Particles of my wife's carbonized womb were inside me now. I hoped to see horror in Dr Phil's eyes but found only psychotic professionalism. He was probably secretly finding the smell appetizing, thinking of ordering his rib-eye *bleu*, as his gloved hands stretched wide the wound, from which emerged two blue and wrinkly feet. It was all happening too fast. The female doctor held the ankles and began to lift. There was no warning. No drum roll. No bugle call. The boy's legs kept coming and coming, legs upon legs. I heard Garthene say my name but it was not possible to look away. This was a must-see. The female doctor was holding the baby by his feet while his head and shoulders remained submerged. With a hooked finger, Dr Phil pulled the arms through and they hung limp and lifeless, which was fine, I reminded myself, because we had been warned that all babies enter a semi-conscious state, almost meditative, for passage through the birth canal. The baby's waxy grey torso was *also* fine because we'd been told about a special word, *vernix*, from Latin, meaning fragrant resin. Fragrant resin. Then the boy's head slid through, displacing pink liquid, wearing his cord like a scarf, and even this was fine because obstetricians unwrap them every single day, routinely, as you or I might untie our shoelaces. *Nothing* was not fine about this limp, grey, offal-smelling, unbreathing thing emerging upside down from a wound that looked like a mouth. Still, it was hard to control my feelings. Everything was different in the flesh, especially the flesh. Jenny said my name more sharply but I could not look away. I was waiting for the cry. No noise could have been more appropriate, but no sound came. Doctor Phil unwound the cord. A nurse I'd not noticed before shoved a blue rubber pipette, a kind of baster, into the baby's mouth in a manner that was perhaps necessarily brisk but felt violent. The baster rasped as it sucked at the back of his throat. There was no cry. There was no jazz piano. The lights in the room darkened. Our underfunded NHS. I had not slept well in weeks. The walls began to narrow. They say this happens to women in the final stages of labour. The room closes in. There is nothing in the world but their body and the child attached by a slug-textured visibly throbbing cord. I went down on one knee to get a more stable centre of gravity. Once I was down there it was hard not to look at the fluids running into the drain in the middle of the room. A little pink stream. It was either beautiful or terrible, I could no longer tell the difference. It would be wrong to say I 'passed out'. I simply decided to cool my cheek against the plastic floor and, as I did so, I heard a small animal whelp that I later learned, with disappointment, came from my own mouth.

That I had failed as a father and husband seemed certain until I saw myself in the wider context of other men on the postnatal ward. Everywhere were new dads, lost and incapable. While the convalescent mothers and babies remained hidden behind the partitioned blue curtains – their pains and joys purely auditory – I joined the useless daddies adrift in the bays, holding bundles of sodden bed sheets, ferrying jugs of tap water, obstructing gangways, constantly peckish, and all wearing shorts and flip-flops and stretched T-shirts because we'd been told the ward would be overheated so that we all looked weirdly surf-ready, but with the wide empty eyes of the drowned.

I filled another jug of water and took it to Garthene. She and my son were not in a room, merely in the idea of a room, a small curtained-off cube of well-lit windowless space that, at any other time, would have seemed profoundly depressing. It was testament to the power of my new son that I found it just fine. Garthene was tilted up beneath thick blankets, an IV in her arm, our perfectly healthy boy on her bare chest. He wasn't blue any more; he was the colour of a hammered thumb, lying face down, locked on to her left nipple as though he'd fallen from the sky and landed there.

Jenny was leaning over the bed, observing the latch. 'How does it feel?' she said.

'Like he's grinding broken glass into my chest,' Garthene said.

'A miracle,' I said.

Jenny had positioned the boy so that his legs wouldn't kick down at Garthene's staples. He lay diagonally across her chest, like a winner's sash.

Just then, Dr Phil appeared at the gap in the curtain, holding sweet, strong tea for both of us. I took the cups from him and told him he was a brilliant genius.

'You're too kind.'

'No,' I said. 'I'm not.'

It was impossible to remember why I had disliked this man.

Once the boy had finished feeding, Jenny held him while I helped Garthene shuffle to the accessible bathroom with a plastic two-pint jug. I waited outside and, after a few minutes, Garthene emerged holding the same jug, but now full of bloody pink urine. We both looked in horror to Jenny who, against all possible expectations, said: 'Well done – that's perfect.' It was a world in opposites.

Time passed at an unsettling speed. The phrase that I had previously regarded as a symptom of repulsive sentimentality – *they grow up so fast* – now seemed brilliantly profound. In just one afternoon I had watched my son change colour, shape and temperament. Now it was seven o'clock and approaching my curfew. I did not want to miss the next thirteen hours. I bent down and kissed Garthene on the mouth. She wasn't able to lean forward and reciprocate because they'd severed all her stomach muscles.

'You are fucking incredible,' I said.

'Thank you.'

There was a little hiccup that, for a moment, I thought with excitement was my son's first hiccup, before I recognized it as her phone receiving a message. She did not read it. Our lives had deepened. I would never check my email again.

'I've got to head back for curfew now, but I'll be first through the gates, tomorrow morning.'

'We'll be here,' she said.

'Can I hold him again?'

'Of course.'

I unbuttoned my shirt, then lifted the sticky baby off her chest and on to mine. For a single gorgeous moment he mistook my nipple for something worth his time. Then he shut his eyes and I watched his face relax into one that was unmistakably my own.

As I walked away, I found it necessary to put a hand on the wall for balance. Maybe it was like how deep-sea divers have to take decompression breaks on their way back to the surface. I stopped a while by obstetrics, watched the midwives chatting behind a long desk. Eventually I made it outside but had to stop in the car park for another breather. That's when I spotted Peter's Vauxhall Astra in the staff bays. It didn't seem right that he should be allowed to remain in the same building as my son and wife while I was on curfew. I went over to have a look at his vehicle. It had quite a number of unsightly scratches on the bodywork. The fact that he didn't feel it necessary to have the car resprayed illustrated his limitless humility. On the back seat, I noticed a cuddly knitted egg with arms and legs. That meant he was already buying toys for my baby. I noticed a pack of WaterWipes in the car door's pocket. Typically, these are used for tending the sensitive skin of newborn children, but I chose to believe his were for other purposes, unrelated to my child. Dusting his dashboard, perhaps, or wiping clean his genitals after having condomless sex with my wife. That wasn't a helpful thought. I shook my head and exhaled a breath that organized nothing.

I needed to sit down and the bonnet of his car was very convenient. I sat hard on it. I got up and did it again, kind of jumped bum-first, making sure to aim for the bonnet's middle, where the metal was most vulnerable. It made a satisfying *wub* sound. I wasn't quite ready to leave the hospital grounds yet, that much was clear. So I decided that I would walk back through the building and out the other exit in order to make my journey home a little longer.

I let myself be led instinctively towards the east wing. It didn't feel like I was planning any of this, but I did approach ICU and it did suddenly seem totally rational to pop in and have a quick, friendly word with Peter, let him know that he should play no further part in our lives.

I told the nurse at reception that I was here to visit my partner and she let me straight in. That was one upside to looking hollow and haggard. She mistook me for a regular. Inside, the ward was much busier than it had been in the night-time. I saw the hospital priest prowling the bays in his robes, smiling and scanning for weakness. At the far end of the ward, I walked slowly past three blue-screened booths, looking for the top of Peter's head through the curtain-rail hoops. When it's really bad news they keep the curtains drawn. It was quieter down this end, too. That suited me fine because I wanted to speak with Peter very softly. A long shadow passed across a curtain and I peered through. He was there, hooking up bags of green and red fluid, as though hanging baubles on a tree.

'Peter,' I whispered, 'Peter. Can I speak to you for a minute?'

He turned, a pouch of clear liquid in his palm.

'Ray,' he said quietly, 'what a surprise. How's it going?'

'Really well,' I said, my voice as soft as a breeze. 'Really, really well.'

'Glad to hear it. Just give me a minute.'

I could barely hear him.

'No problem at all.'

We were trying to out-whisper each other.

Through the gap in the curtain, I could see a young man in the bed, his eyes open, texting. He had a drip in each arm and an oxygen probe, like a clothes peg, clamped to the tip of his right forefinger. Apart from that, he looked perfectly alert and healthy. It's the ones with no visible damage who are in the most trouble. Peter slid aside the curtain and stepped out, shook my hand with great accuracy.

'Garthene's got our beautiful little boy asleep on her chest,' I said.

'That's wonderful,' he said.

'I just wanted to give you the good news in person. He looks just like me.'

'I'm so pleased,' he said, and he did sound pleased. 'They say they come out looking like their dads.'

'That's right,' I said.

It was clear by his steady smile that Peter had not been haunted by questions of possible paternity. Behind him, the patient's motorized bed was very gently yawing, battling bedsores. He glanced at my scrubs, all crinkled from where they'd put me in the recovery position.

'And how did you find the birth?'

'A*maz*ing,' I said.

'That's great,' he said. 'Because I know a lot of people find it challenging.'

'I didn't,' I said. 'But I appreciate your empathy.'

'Some men pretend childbirth isn't difficult when, in truth – without ever going to war – witnessing a Caesarian can be the single most traumatic experience of their lives.'

'Ha ha.'

'We treat quite a few new fathers for PTSD.'

'I did not know that but thank you for the information.'

'Don't be too proud to ask for help is all I'm saying. There's support if you need it.'

'I won't need it.'

'Okay good,' he said. 'You go get some sleep.'

I put the palm of my hand on Peter's chest and told him not to fucking patronize me. I said it so nicely.

Peter did not react. I could feel his heart through his chest.

'What time does your shift end, old pal?' I said.

'Technically, two hours ago,' he said.

'I see,' I said. 'The thing is, I have to go home for curfew now, but I don't feel comfortable leaving you alone in the same building as my wife and newborn.'

It felt good to be honest.

As he looked into my eyes, I could sense him listing my pathologies. Call it what you will, I felt wonderfully alive.

Behind one of the curtains, machines began to chirp. The birdsong of bloodwork. New dawn in the city of death.

Peter offered to drive me home. He changed into his civilian clothes – navy chinos and a bright yellow T-shirt – and we walked out together. I stayed just a couple of paces behind him, the most disconcerting distance. His strides were too long. For every four, I needed five.

We got into his car and went slowly out of the car park. He drove as though there were a newborn on board. Even on the Lower Clapton Road, he kept to the actual speed limit, twenty miles an hour. Nobody drives at that speed. It's just an idea. Reflections of street lights slid through the dent on his bonnet, which Peter noticed but did not mention. As we approached a pedestrian crossing, the light turned amber and any normal person would have pushed on through, but Peter braked steadily, not a stamp but a squeeze, and the car halted without even engaging our seat belts. The sky was dimming and I needed to clear up a few things.

'Why did you sleep with my wife?' I said.

Peter stared, listening to the beeps. 'I know it's not enough, but I'm truly sorry,' he said.

'It's not nearly enough,' I said.

'I feel terrible about it. We both do.'

'Don't say *we*.'

Peter pulled smoothly away. His driving dictated the pace of the conversation.

'There's something I've been wondering,' I said.

'Okay.'

'And I feel I have a right to know.'

'Go ahead.'

'Did you and Garthene use a condom?'

Peter fed the wheel, turned a corner. I felt the weight of his respectability with each click of his indicators.

'Yes,' he said. 'We used one.'

He didn't realize that *not* using one was the right answer.

We drove on for a while. He pulled out wide around a helmet-less cyclist. What would it take to make this man lose control? I grabbed the colourful knitted toy egg from the back seat and propped it up in my lap.

'Nice of you to buy a present for my little boy.'

'Ray, that's my daughter's.'

'Oh, sure it is, and what's her name?'

'Melina.'

'Me*li*na,' I said, in an incredulous voice, though in truth I already knew he was not lying.

'It's a German name. Her mother's German.' Then he eased his phone from his trouser pocket, unlocked it with his left hand, opened the photos and handed it to me – all without taking his eyes off the road. I looked at a picture of a cute toddler dressed as a skeleton. 'She's four,' he said.

I swiped left, past photos of his adorable daughter attempting cartwheels, posing among double-jointed cacti. I saw no pictures of anyone who might be Melina's mother, and that seemed an opportunity.

'Are you and the German mother still together?'

'Unfortunately not. We're divorced.'

A police van overtook us, momentarily filling the car with light and noise.

'Sorry, I didn't catch that,' I said, just to make him say it again.

'We're divorced,' he said.

'That's a shame.' I swung my head back and forth extravagantly. 'That's a huge shame.'

'We didn't have a good relationship,' he said.

'Right,' I said, 'so your daughter was a mistake?'

'No.'

'Oh, so you *intended* to bring a child into your horrible lives?'

We were below the speed limit. It would have been faster to run.

'I guess so,' he said.

'And why was that?' I said.

'We wanted a baby.'

He clicked on his headlights, though it was still light enough to see. I scrolled through some more photos – Melina riding a doggy, Melina in the ball pool – then I decided to explore the other parts of his phone. I looked at his text messages but could only see names I didn't recognize.

'Your kid is a*dor*able,' I said, as I looked for his other messaging apps. I opened Telegram, the Russian-designed one that drug dealers and adulterers use because of the end-to-end encryption. And there I saw my wife's name beside a red marker: two new messages.

Peter glanced over now. I angled the screen away from him.

'She's so photogenic,' I said.

The messages were only five minutes old. The first one was a picture in which Garthene was topless but that wasn't what made it upsetting. There was a man asleep against her breasts but that wasn't what made it upsetting. She had waited for me to leave, then sent this image to Peter from her hospital bed. What's worse, she was smiling. I knew a whole lot about hateable smiles and had never seen one worse.

The message read: *You still around? xx*

I let the phone fall from my hand into the footwell.

Then what else was there to do but punch the dashboard? I punched it once and then again, punched the plastic hood that covered the stereo, and felt nothing.

Peter stopped the car in the middle of the road and peered down at the screen of his phone. Then he frowned and looked at me. Something passed his eyes, and I had a horrible feeling it was pity.

'Please,' I said. 'I'm begging you. Just leave us alone.'

'I will,' he said.

'You won't,' I said, and I thumped the dashboard again. Not easy to get a good backswing from where I was, but I found an angle.

He watched me.

I hit the dashboard again and this time my knuckle split.

'Keep going,' he said.

I kept going.

'Harder.'

I went harder, leaving a red smear on the plastic.

'Here,' he said. He offered his face towards me and closed his eyes. 'Do your worst.'

I really wanted to do my worst. But I had a vision of how the bruises would work with his cheekbones, how he would drive back to the hospital, neatly three-point-turning – or five-point, or seven, just to be safe – then head to obstetrics, soft-talk his way in after visiting hours, wave away any offer of treatment, get Garthene upgraded to a side room and set up a camp bed beside her, the three of them waking together, my first son's first sunrise, witnessed in the shadow of this tall god in chinos.

'Hit me,' he said, his eyes still closed.

I let my fist move straight past his face. I had no conscious plan but was pleased with my deep brain when I reached around the steering wheel and tugged the key from the ignition.

I got out of the car and crossed the road. Only once Peter's eyes were open did I let the key slip from my fingers into the drain, fall into Victorian darkness, a splash far below. That was all the vengeance I could summon. Those modern keys cost a lot to replace.

It was seven forty-five when I got to Dave's. I had missed a call from Serco and I rang them back immediately.

'Sorry,' I said.

'Mr Morris, do you know what time it is?'

'It was because of the birth of my son. A beautiful boy.'

'You should have told us.'

'I know. I'm so sorry. It was a complicated birth.'

'I do know how these things can be,' the man from Serco said.

'Thank you for being understanding.'

'I'm a father too. You're going to love it.'

'Okay.'

'Are your wife and son still in hospital?'

'They are. They'll be there all night without me.'

'Don't worry. You have a good sleep while you can. You'll need it!'

'Ha ha ha, thank you.'

'Enjoy it, pal. It's the most beautiful thing in the world.'

'I will.'

I ended the call and stared at the phone. Serco were so friendly. I looked up and Dave was watching from the door to his room.

'Do I see a father before me?' he said.

We hugged in the living room. Then Allen appeared in the doorway and though I'd never met him before, the fact of my being a father overrode all social coolness and we hugged too. I stayed in the hug until I began to cry. I had cried more times in the last month than in the last decade. I was a crier now. The town crier.

'Are you okay?' Dave said.

'I'm fine. I'm happy.'

'You should be.'

'I am.'

I released Allen and went to the fridge and opened it, basked in the bleak light, the cool air calming my cheeks. *Expecting Everything* had recommended I do a big shop before the baby was born because I wouldn't have time afterwards. I'd gone to the posh grocer's where the staff are truly happy and the rough wooden walls recall an alpine lodge and they pack everything into big, impractical paper bags. I'd bought three gold-foil-embossed bottles of rosé, a black-legged chicken, pink fir potatoes, heirloom onions and a huge Amalfi lemon which I had sniffed, handsomely, while they told me how much it would all cost.

I picked the lemon out now. It was the same size as my son's skull. I took big breaths off its nubbin, as though breathing Entonox. There was no need to think of Peter walking all the way back to the hospital and telling my wife what I had done with his car key, or worse, not telling her – just saying, *Don't worry, everything's fine, Ray got home safe* – and she knowing by his eyes that everything wasn't fine, that I had done something irresponsible, but that he was protecting her from it because of how much he loved her.

I halved the lemon and shoved it into the chicken's cavity. There was some blood on my knuckles from where I'd punched the dashboard. I put butter on my fingers and pushed it under the skin of the breasts. When you pay a lot of money for a chicken they let you keep the innards. Neck, heart, liver, all pressed together in a little vacuum-sealed bag. It occurred to me that I had never even seen the placenta. By the time I woke up, they had whisked it away to be incinerated. I thought of how the Igbo consider the placenta the deceased twin of the baby and conduct full funeral rites. I thought of the hospital's narrow smokestack exhaling carbonized offcuts. I thought of how some hospitals have a special machine that converts the burning of human remains into energy to heat the wards. The overly warm room where my child was now sleeping on my wife.

I chopped onions to legitimize my crying. While I was doing that, Dave and Allen sat on the sofa and chatted too quietly for me to hear. Dave made Allen laugh and when he laughed he threw his head back and when his head went back it revealed his elegant neck and when Dave saw that he felt compelled to kiss it and make little clucky noises which made Allen laugh again, so on and so on, the two of them carrying each other to paradise.

I washed the potatoes and dug out the eyes. The chicken was in the oven and every so often I used Dave's baster to slurp up and redistribute the fat at the bottom of the roasting tray. To open the oven door and feel the rush of hot air fill my nostrils and throat with the smell of cooking flesh was almost too evocative. I was well into the second bottle of rosé by the time I brought the food out.

Allen had a wonderful sitting posture. He wore a pale blue blouse and a string of low-slung pearls, his hair tied back in a stubby, Japanese-style ponytail. Dave wore a vintage French work jacket. They were dressed for a celebration.

'Well, congratulations again!' Dave said, raising his drink.

'Thank you!' I said. 'My son is the most gorgeous thing in the world!'

Our glasses chimed together, each one playing a note marginally different from the others, creating a discordant, woozy ringing, like after you've been punched. Even as they took a sip, they watched each other through the glass. Whatever they had, I wanted it.

'It's nice to finally meet you, Allen,' I said.

'You too,' he said.

I whispered to him from behind my hand, 'You're every bit as fit as Dave promised.'

'Ray, keep it civil,' Dave said.

Allen laughed, touched Dave's arm. 'Let the man speak!' he said.

'Dave said you are the most exquisite creature in the world,' I said, 'and he was right.'

Allen blushed and I was glad. I took a long drink and decided that I was discovering something new about myself.

'But Dave,' I said, 'you're also very attractive.'

'Take a deep breath, Ray,' Dave said.

'What?' I said. 'Are heterosexual new fathers not allowed to appreciate male beauty?'

Allen covered his mouth as he laughed.

'Just try not to be creepy,' Dave said.

I gave them drumsticks because I wanted to see them eat with their hands. The chicken was unbelievably delicious. We ate it in silence, just the chewing noises and the smell. There was a pop as I opened the third bottle. Dave looked at me.

'Slow down,' he said.

'I don't want to.'

Dave gave me a hard stare that forced me to get up and clear the table. I stacked our plates and cutlery and went to the other side of the room, the kitchenette, put the dishes in the sink. I washed up slowly, luxuriantly, not so much scrubbing the plates as letting my hand be guided by the contours. I was working hard to keep the mood going. I liked the little squeaky noises. I gently rubbed my crotch against the cupboard below the sink.

By the time I was done, they were putting their coats on.

'I think we're going to go out for last orders,' Dave said.

'No,' I said. 'Please don't go. We're having fun. There's still most of a bottle of blush.'

'You have it.'

'Please don't leave me alone,' I said.

'Come to the pub with us,' Allen said.

'I'd love to, but I'm not allowed outside after dark because of my' – I tried to say it in a light-hearted way – 'criminal conviction.'

'Oh, man,' Allen said. 'I forgot about that.'

Dave's expression was blank and I sensed he had a plan to get away from me.

'Stay for just one more drink,' I said. 'I'll be completely normal.'

'Ha ha,' Allen said, 'I don't mind staying for one –'

'We're meeting friends,' Dave said and he held the door open.

'Right,' I said. 'You better go. Don't worry if you want to bring your friends back later.'

Dave ignored me and went out into the hallway.

Even before the door clicked shut, I was drinking another glass of crisp, cool rosé. It was ten o'clock. That was lights-out time for my wife and son in the hospital. I paced around the edges of the flat, following the walls, the limits of my freedom. I thought about calling Garthene, but I knew she needed rest. I imagined Peter there, beyond visiting hours, watching my son breathe.

The wine ran out.

I got up, went through the cupboards and found some raki, a tourist's bottle half-wrapped in wicker. I swigged it and let some run down my chest. I stood in Dave's room, inhaling. I lay on the mattress on the floor. On his bedside table I saw another vial of the same drugs that had fallen from his pocket at the picnic. I put nine drops into the raki. I poured out two glasses and put them on the bedside table with a note: *Hope you had fun. Here's a nightcap xxx.* Spiking my friends' drinks with an aphrodisiac was a massive aphrodisiac.

I turned off the lights and lay in the corner of the lounge with my eyes closed, but I couldn't sleep. When I opened my laptop, the browser's tabs held well-lit medical videos of every kind of unexpected birth – ruptures, breeches, ineffective epidurals – accompanied by all kinds of glottal-stopped throat noises and elaborate breathing, so I slammed the laptop shut. I opened Dave's computer and searched for hard gay porn. Most videos lacked discernible narrative, but I found some that were about straight men realizing the truth about themselves, how their lives were a lie and they would have to tell their families. The straight guys generally wore baseball caps. I owned one of those. My favourite video was about this cute boy called Kevin who was paying for his traditional church wedding by sucking all available cocks. His clients came all over his face and called it a bridal veil. I took my top off. I had most of an erection. It was clear I would have to tell Garthene, explain that all my life's mistakes stemmed from the suppression of my true sexuality, but that I was coming to terms with it. I went into the bathroom, which was a wet room. I cleaned my teeth with Dave's electric toothbrush, brushing hard, watching the foam build at the corners of my lips.

When Allen and Dave came in at four in the morning, I'd finished all the raki but for the two glasses on their bedside table and I was lying very still and naked in the dark of the lounge, concentrating. I heard them lower their voices in the hall. They stepped shoeless into Dave's room, activating some of the floorboards. They made sympathetic noises as they read my note. They gently clinked their glasses, then shushed each other, then laughed at their inability to be shushed. I crawled on all fours towards the strip of light at the bottom of Dave's door, brought my face close enough to see their feet on the other side, still in socks. I felt the presence of their hard bodies, their non-reproductive love-making. The slithery noise of a belt yanked through its loops before it dropped, half coiled, on the floor.

I stood up slowly, put my hand to the door and pushed. Light repainted me. I had no muscles, but some people are into that. The room was lit by a single lamp on the floor. Dave was sitting on the edge of the mattress, his head right back, neck gorgeously exposed, squeezing the vial of sex drugs into his eyeballs, flinching slightly as the drops hit home. It was possible that the vial contained eye drops, not stimulants, but, by this point, it didn't matter. Allen was standing, topless, with a glass of raki in his hand.

I stepped into the doorway. 'You can do whatever you want to me,' I said.

'Ray?' Allen said.

I took another step.

Dave shook his head and said: 'Fuck's sake.'

Allen slowly put down his glass of raki and, without taking his eyes off me, picked up a large red beach towel off the floor. He held it out wide and took careful steps towards me, matador-style, then wrapped the towel around my waist, tied it behind me, all without making any meaningful physical contact.

Dave blinked away moisture from his eyes.

Together, they laid me down in the middle of the mattress. I felt a waft of cool air when they lowered the sheet on top of me, as one might give decency to a corpse. They clicked off the light and I heard their footsteps retreat.

'Please don't go,' I said.

'We'll just be next door,' Allen said.

'Don't leave me.'

There was a pause. 'We'll keep the door open,' Dave said.

'Just sleep beside me. You don't need to worry. I won't try anything.'

There was a long wait, a really long wait, enough time for them to communicate to each other with their eyes that this would soon be an amusing memory. I was their future anecdote, I knew that now.

I felt the mattress shift as they sat either side of me on the bed.

It was a mild night and they slept on top of the sheet, both in T-shirts and boxer shorts. It was a threesome, of sorts, and I completed some deep internal list and let it evaporate. I was surprised and impressed by how quickly their breathing thickened. Soon they were both snoring gently, their rhythms mismatched. I allowed myself to believe that we could live like this for ever. That each night I could crawl into bed between them. Like a dog. Or a child.

PART FIVE

Meet Bobby, my perfect son. He has a cold and we are on a bus. He keeps inflating a small, snail-shaped bubble from his left nostril. And as it pops – it pops! – not only is it audible, the moment of air escaping, but it changes form entirely, the snot, becoming this dense thing that could be used to seal a decree. *I hereby declare my son perfect only to me.*

Today is a handover day. Bobby and I have an hour remaining in each other's company and I like to make sure that he is truly exhausted and tetchy before I return him to Garthene and Peter. He's wearing a T-shirt I bought that says: *Daddy doesn't want your advice.*

We get off at Leyton High Road and browse a shop that sells extortionate three-wheeled prams with disc brakes. 'Hi, gorgeous,' says the beautiful shop assistant, speaking only to my nine-month-old son in his front-facing papoose. A father's testosterone levels drop drastically after the birth of his first child. It's a relief to be saved from my rudimentary cravings. I ask her how much the most expensive buggy costs – a design based on a 1950s Buick – then I nod at the answer before saying that I'll talk to my wife about it. Joke's on her, I'm single.

After that, Bobby and I stand outside the window display of

Mothercare. We come here every Thursday to see baby Lydia. Or baby Lucy. Whichever. She's on a huge poster. Twenty times her actual size, raised to the weight and height of a grizzly bear, wearing workman's dungarees.

'Once upon a time, your daddy was on a big poster, just like this,' I tell him. 'But he didn't get paid a penny.'

He swings an open palm at the poster in what I take for disgust. I bring our faces close to the window so that we can breathe condensation against the glass until the spoiled child disappears.

Around the corner from Peter and Garthene's new flat, I sit on a bench in a park and help Bobby drink. Each week, Garthene hands me pouches of expressed and frozen breast milk. Nowadays, this is the most intimate part of our marriage. I like to feel the weight of them and, once they are defrosted, taste their surprising sweetness, each batch slightly different. Some are thin and watery but today's has a clear band of cream on top.

'Hind milk,' I tell Bobby. 'Hind milk.'

As Bobby drinks, I admire his scalp, which is covered in waxy, cornflaky scales. He has seborrhoeic dermatitis, or, to use the disturbing colloquial term, cradle cap. Nobody would wear caps if they resembled seborrhoeic dermatitis, yet I find it endearing. It takes effort to resist picking the flakes off and eating them. With a few drops of Garthene's breast milk, I could make a tiny, emotional breakfast.

It's quarter to one. There's just enough time to lie on the short grass and let Bobby attack me. He rakes my nostrils with his sharp fingernails, prods my eyes and strikes me, open-palmed, again and again, across my nose bridge. One of life's true pleasures. The more wounded I sound, the happier he gets and the faster he hits me, and so the more noises I make. Onward, upward, the two of us in perfect sadomasochistic union, until he is laughing and slapping, slapping and laughing, while I howl at the sky. A young and obviously childless couple are judging us from the entrance to the park. Bobby and I are not remotely embarrassed. In fact, we get off on their watching.

At one o'clock exactly, I strap Bobby to my chest like a bomb then head to Garthene and Peter's grim, mostly basement-level flat, which they own. Even though it is small and damp, it must have stretched their nurses' salaries, and it's hard to get away from the thought that they are in crippling debt together, and what could be more romantic. Bobby and I do fly-bys of Peter's Astra. The dent in the bonnet has still not been sucked flat.

'Don't crash,' I tell Bobby, as he banks hard, laughing wildly, clipping the wing mirror with the soles of his knitted booties. There's now a pleasing note of desperation in Bobby's happiness, laughter as a prelude to something bleaker, sadder, more permanent.

'Hi, Ray,' says a voice behind me.

I give Bobby one final, slow orbit of the Astra, vibrating him in my hands, making his laughter judder while I do the rocket noise. 'Approaching destination,' I say, in a robot voice. 'Population: two, possibly human. Atmosphere: self-satisfied.'

I let Bobby's laughter fade before I take the three slow steps down the stairs to the basement front door so that, by the bottom, my son is silent and there's a melancholy weight inside him that I know won't shift.

'Here you go,' I say.

'Hello, handsome,' Peter says.

'Earn,' Bobby says. 'Urn.'

His first word was either *earn* or *urn* or, I'd like to believe, an intentional play on both *earn* and *urn*, illustrating his central theme that wealth cannot forestall death.

Peter thanks me and shuts the door behind him. Through the strip of wire-reinforced glass, I see Peter stop and tug a tissue from his back pocket, wet it between his lips. I know he is going to clear away the crusted greenish snot from around my son's nostrils. He always wants to clean him up, his love is that shallow. I see the swing of Peter's elbow as he tries to wipe in a swift and light-hearted way, but Bobby will always call him out on his bullshit. As they disappear from sight, there is pleasure in hearing a rising noise, the tremulous wail of my son's true sorrow. My darling bomb.

Above us, Garthene is crouching at the slightly open bedroom window beside Melina, Peter's daughter, who I like a lot more than him.

'You remember Ray?' Garthene says to Melina. 'Ray is Bobby's daddy.'

I wave. Garthene and Peter are completely honest with the children about our disastrous adult relationships.

'And you're Bobby's mummy?' the girl says.

'That's right.'

Garthene looks haggard from sleeplessness, cheeks hanging loose from her face. The more broken she looks, the more I think we should be together. She has her hair cut boy-short. Just a little swipe at the front, shaved at the sides. It looks uneven and I can tell Peter cut it himself, mapping her head with clippers, an intimacy I will never know. She turns her head to listen to a sound from downstairs. Bobby is in full meltdown now, his screams entering their second stage, more raspy, dry and quivery. Peter has many undeniable qualities but, in this case, I feel certain only a blood relative can bring Bobby comfort. I watch this realization pass across Garthene's face before she disappears from view.

It's just me and Melina now. She has brown curls and a notable forehead. The windows have stoppers so that she can't throw herself out.

'Why is Bobby always crying?' Melina says, bringing her face to the gap.

'Because he doesn't like your daddy,' I say.

'Why doesn't he like my daddy?'

'Could be any number of things.'

There's always this weightlessness, once Bobby's gone. A son-shaped hole in the middle of my chest. For this reason, I like to plan my Thursday afternoons carefully, because otherwise it's easy to spiral. I am on my way to meet Marie and Lee at a pub called O'Malley's. We are friends again because it's hard to make meaningful new relationships when you're over thirty.

I walk along the canal wearing shorts, showing off the skin where my ankle tag used to be. A little patch of hairless innocence glowing in the sunshine, if it were sunny, which it isn't. It's another kind of weather I don't care to record.

At the back of the pub, they have a big drink waiting for me on a small round table. I'd always assumed this pub was just Irish-themed, but now I know it is real. The landlady is called Mhairi and she's from Galway. There are gloomy booths along one wall, Chinese students doing karaoke in the back room, a screen showing Gaelic football, and another, bigger screen for football.

We glug down pints of strong, bland lager – 'Mhairi, which is the one that tastes of nothing?' – then move to whisky. There must be UV light somewhere because I can see layers of sun damage on Lee and Marie's faces, submerged freckles, sunspots. It gives Marie a lovely, almost supernatural look, as though all her younger selves are with her, fading back into the skull. Lee's head soon turns its ripest colour and we start playing a game, retelling each other's traumatic life events as if they are our own.

'Did I ever tell you about the time I found my wife in bed with one of our closest friends?' I say.

'I don't think you did,' Lee says. 'Sounds awful!'

'It was!' I say. 'So I'm downstairs at one of our parties and I'm thinking I haven't seen my wife in a while.'

'Uh-oh,' Lee says.

'Then on the landing I hear her voice calling "Lee-bo!"' As I sing his name, I watch Lee's jaw tighten. ' "Lee-bo, I'm in bed with this average-looker and absolutely parched." '

'I hope you decked the guy,' Lee says.

'Don't worry. I smacked him. Down he went. Like a baby!'

'Like a baby!' Marie says.

Lee turns away to let his gaze be calmed by the big screen, a heat-map infographic rotating in his eyes. Marie leans over and puts her head on his shoulder.

'Honey, why don't you tell the one about the time you didn't have a baby?'

'You really want to hear that one?' Lee says.

'I do,' she says.

'Did I ever tell you about when I didn't have a baby?' Lee says.

'I don't think you did,' I say.

He turns over an empty whisky glass. Then he takes Marie's right hand and together they start moving the glass around the circular wooden table, in the manner of a Ouija board, as though communing with the dead. The glass pushes beer slops on to the carpet and some on to my leg, which they don't notice

and I don't mention. It takes me a moment to realize they are mim-
ing an ultrasound. Then Lee takes his hands off the glass.

'Is there anything wrong, doctor?' Lee says.

'I'm afraid, ma'am, we can't find a heartbeat,' Marie says in her
medical voice, which is American.

'Can't find a heartbeat?' Lee says. 'I'm no obstetrician but that
doesn't sound good!'

I realize I have never heard this story before.

'Ma'am,' Marie says, 'I'm sorry to say a heartbeat is a total must-
have, baby-wise.' She puts her ear to Lee's stomach. 'And it's
utterly barren in there.'

'Desolate as the tundra!' Lee says.

'No, hang on – wait,' Marie says. 'I hear gurgling!'

'Oh, that's just my stomach acid!' Lee says, and they both laugh.

Lee lifts up Marie's hand – the right one, ringless – and he kisses
each knuckle in turn, which at first seems cheesy and over-
demonstrative but by the last knuckle has achieved a transcendent
privacy. Marie sits up and they kiss with tongues. They keep kissing
for long enough that I find it necessary to look away and contem-
plate the history of the Irish-themed pub. How the companies who
built Irish bars in Dubai, Bangkok and Vancouver, in malls and
airport lounges, then recognized Ireland as a viable market. So
they opened Irish-themed pubs in Dublin and Galway and they
did well. It turns out that the Irish enjoy having a drink inside a
fantasy about themselves, and who wouldn't? So the Irish-themed
pubs in Caracas and Johannesburg have become authentic, retrospectively, an honest representation of the homeland, whereas pubs
like this one, run by actual Irish, lack the true flavour.

Marie and Lee are still going.

'Marie,' I say, knocking on the table with my knuckles, 'why don't you tell us about the time your wife left you for a tall, dependable and recently divorced ICU nurse?'

They stop kissing. She smooths her skirt. Lee turns the whisky glass upright.

'Not much to tell. Throughout her pregnancy, I made a series of poor decisions and she just understood this guy was a way better bet.'

'A steady-day-by-day-realization-that-she'd-be-happier-with-him-than-with-you-type thing?' I say.

'Very much so,' she says. 'And I completely respect that decision.'

'No offence,' I say, 'but she definitely upgraded!'

'True,' Marie says, 'and what's more, they even asked for my approval before they bought a place together.'

'Wow, that's extremely, almost psychotically, thoughtful,' I say.

'They wanted to make certain I felt stable, emotionally, before embarking upon their lifetime of loving sex and domestic equality.'

'And when they finally did move in together, were you ready, emotionally?'

'Absolutely not, but I told them that I was,' she says, 'which was a victory.'

'Nice one,' I say.

Lee smiles, his neat teeth in the UV throbbing in his gums. We lift our glasses, drink to our damage. I never imagined for one moment that we could feel at once so broken and so at peace. Then the football ends and all the football-watching people exit the pub, leaving only those of us with a deeper commitment.

It is dark when we head outside, arms round each other's shoulders. In the car park, we see three children strapped in the back of a green people carrier. Standing outside it are their pink-headed parents in khaki shorts, both agreeing that he is under the drink-driving limit.

'You're fine.'

'I'm fine.'

'You're fine.'